# The Fool: New Beginnings

VAL TOBIN

ISBN: 978-1-988609-15-7

# DEDICATION

To everyone who endured lockdowns throughout the COVID pandemic. May reading add pleasure to your life.

To Bob, Jenn, Mark, Chanelle, Savannah, and Jack, always.

## Books in the *Tales from the Unmasqued World* Series

The Fool: New Beginnings
The Magician: Infinity's End
The High Priestess: Persephone's Return
The Empress: A Promise of Rain

# ACKNOWLEDGMENTS

Thank you to Alis B. Kennedy, PhD; Wendy Quirion;
Val Cseh; John Erwin; Michelle Legere; and Diane
King for beta reading, professional advice, and
suggestions.
Editing by Tahlia Newland tahlianewland.com. Thank
you, Tahlia.
Thanks to Patti Roberts of Paradox
(paradoxbooktrailerproductions.blogspot.com.au/)
for the amazing cover.

.

# CHAPTER 1

The lycanthrope, recognizable by the brown wolf pin on her lapel, browsed among the bookshelves at the back of Crossroads Books & Café. She selected a book from the self-help section and, after reading the back cover, flipped through the pages. The rest of the shop was empty of customers, so Kelsey Davis, who stood behind the food counter, glanced often at the young wolf woman.

She wasn't nervous alone in here with a lycan, Kelsey assured herself. She'd naturally monitor any customer browsing through the store. What if the woman needed help? Anyone on staff must remain vigilant, especially when it was quiet.

Wolf Woman raised her head and locked gazes with Kelsey. "I can smell your fear."

Living in denial was so much more difficult when others pointed out the obvious.

"I'm sorry." Kelsey didn't know what else to say. After a moment, she added, "I don't get many lycans in here. At least, I think I don't."

"You're the new owner, I take it?" Wolf Woman replied.

"As of two months ago." Kelsey picked up a spray bottle and a clean rag and moved from behind the counter to wipe down tables—tables that didn't need it, but she had to keep busy to tamp down her fear. Cleaning always worked to distract her and calm her nerves.

"Never met a lycan before?" The woman, who Kelsey decided didn't look so intimidating after all in her pale-green blouse and jeans, returned the book to the shelf and approached the food counter. Her black hair was tied, sleek and smooth, into a bun. If the wolf insignia hadn't signaled her lycan heritage, her aquiline nose, square jaw, and tall, muscular build would've hinted at it. Her flawless skin held a tinge of brown. She prowled rather than walked, but with a model's grace.

The sudden move in Kelsey's direction flipped the fear switch on again, and she took an inadvertent step backward.

"Relax. I just want to introduce myself." Wolf Woman stopped a safe distance away. "I'm Laura Growley."

Deadpan, Kelsey said, "A lycan named Growley."

Laura chuckled. "No weirder than a human named Smith or Miller."

Laura spoke correctly—family names for humans typically reflected what their ancestors did. Perhaps when lycans shifted to the earth plane, they were assigned similarly descriptive names. That was probably the case for all hypernaturals who'd joined the physical plane during the unmasquing.

"Kelsey Davis. You know, I never thought about

naming conventions much before." Something occurred to her then, and any residual fear vanished, replaced by curiosity. "Did you know Mr. Dobbs? The previous owner? Are you a regular here?" If so, it wouldn't hurt to act polite. The effort didn't even feel forced. Laura seemed nice, and if Dobbs had welcomed her into the store, then odds were good it was safe for Kelsey to do the same.

"Yes. I enjoy reading. You have an excellent selection of lycan-centered fiction and non-fiction." She grinned, revealing straight, even teeth.

*What did you expect? Fangs?* No, the fangs would only appear when she changed to wolf form, something Kelsey would happily skip witnessing.

"I'll have a latte, if you don't mind."

The request brought Kelsey back to the real world, one of customer service and business. Her nerves settled, and after asking Laura what size she wanted, Kelsey hurried behind the counter to fill the order.

As she steamed the milk, the bell on the door jingled, signaling another customer's arrival. Voices chattering told her a group had entered, and they were young. Kelsey threw a glance their way and verified it was the teens who visited the café two or three times a week. They hadn't been in for four days, and she beamed a smile at them the instant she recognized them.

Chairs scraped against the floor as the kids settled into their usual table with their usual exuberant bustle. As Kelsey handed Laura the latte, their gazes locked, and Kelsey noticed the tiny lines around Laura's eyes and lips. Lycans rarely suffered from dry skin, making their ages difficult to gauge, so this one had to be close to Kelsey in age—early forties at least—even though she looked no older than thirty.

"Thanks." Laura accepted the large takeout cup. She found an empty table near the counter and pulled a book from the oversized purse she carried, while the group of teens crowded up to the cash register.

The group's orders distracted Kelsey at first, but as she put together a cappuccino for the last teen, she did a quick head count and came up short. The guy before her had waited patiently while the other three members of his group, two girls and another boy, had received their orders. An additional member of their group, a pretty girl with pale skin and golden hair, was absent.

"Where's Dakota?" Kelsey asked, more to make conversation than out of any serious interest. She assumed the girl was busy with a part-time job, family, school—anything at all, really.

"Don't know." His serious tone made her pause and meet his gaze. He frowned, his eyes pinched with worry.

She set his muffin and coffee on the counter. "Everything okay with her?"

He shrugged and averted his gaze, reddening slightly, as if embarrassed at exposing his concern.

"It's all right. If something's wrong, you can tell me."

He threw a glance over his shoulder at the group around the table. "Not sure. Last time we spoke, she sounded kinda worried about her mom."

"Is her mother ill?" Kelsey could relate to that. Her own mother had recently battled cancer. They'd ended up calling in a hedge witch to help her heal completely. Having magickals in the vicinity had its advantages. If Dakota's mother was ill, perhaps Kelsey could refer the witch she and her mother used.

"No." He glanced again at the others, who chatted away, oblivious to the serious conversation taking place at the food counter. "She thought her mother might …" He drifted off, unable or unwilling to give voice to his friend's troubles.

"I know it's not my business, Troy," Kelsey said. "But you're regulars here. I've gotten to know all of you since I took over this place." Or as much as a shopkeeper could get to know her regular customers. She didn't categorize any of the patrons who visited the store as friends. "If something happened to Dakota, maybe I can help." Kelsey's son hung out with that group. She'd ask him later if he knew anything, but for now, she'd try to get information from this boy. She was sure he was on the verge of sharing.

The bell jingled again as the door opened. Chase, the young man Kelsey had hired to work evenings and weekends in the café, rushed inside.

"Sorry, just made it. I'll drop my gear and be right over." He raced through the store and into the staff room at the back.

If Troy had been ready to divulge Dakota's personal problems, Chase's entrance had changed his mind.

"I'm sure it's nothing." He picked up his coffee and muffin. "Thanks." With a nod, he retreated to the safety of the group.

Frustrated at the interruption, but unable to do anything about it, Kelsey returned to wiping surfaces that didn't need cleaning. When Chase appeared behind the counter, she smiled and welcomed him with an upbeat greeting. "How was your day?"

"Good. Busy. Exams soon."

Chase was in college, studying to be a mage. She'd never understood why someone with natural-born magickal ability had to study it in school, but he'd explained that innate talent was only the beginning. Magick had levels of complexity it would take him years of study to master.

"I see the gang's all here." He did a double-take. "I stand corrected. The dhampir girl's missing."

"What?" *Dhampir.* She should know what that meant.

Chase raised his brows and angled his head at her. "Dakota. She never displayed the insignia prominently, but she kept it with her. Even so, her pedigree is unmistakable. She's a human-vampire mixed breed."

"I didn't know that. I didn't see it." Should she have noticed? All this time, the girl had seemed so normal. "I never saw fangs."

Chase patted her arm. "Don't worry about it. Humans have trouble recognizing them—until the fangs appear or they notice the lack of an image on a reflective surface. They're nothing to be afraid of, you know."

"I'm not afraid of them." But she averted her eyes as she said it, and inside, she had the uneasy feeling she lied to herself as much as to Chase.

The bell on the door tinkled again. Two men strolled in. She'd been expecting them, since they showed up at this time each month. They weren't here to buy coffee, though they expected her to serve them. She pressed a button that popped open her till. After lifting the tray inside, she retrieved an envelope containing $500 and handed it to the taller of the two men. He was always the one who took the money while the other man remained standing by the door.

The tall man shoved the envelope into the inside pocket of his trench coat and waited while she fixed two cappuccinos to go. When she handed those over, the men strolled out without having exchanged a word with her. She preferred it that way, and they didn't seem to care as long as she paid them when they showed up.

A craving for a hit of caffeine assaulted her, and she poured herself a large coffee. She might regret it when she wanted to sleep later, but right now, she needed the comforting warmth of hot liquid and the reassuring caffeine buzz. She glanced over at Laura, who appeared to be snout deep in her book. Ashamed she'd referred to the lycan's nose as a snout even though she was in human form, Kelsey shifted her gaze to Chase.

He'd busied himself with sweeping behind the counter while the goons were in the store, but now he paused to look her in the eyes. "Someone should do something about those guys."

She shook her head, afraid he considered playing hero. "No. Stay out of it." She kept her voice low, and verified with a glance that Laura continued reading and the group of kids remained oblivious to what had transpired.

Before Chase could reply, the bells jangled and clashed as the door burst open, and a man wearing the vampire insignia on his lapel stepped inside. Time to prove to Chase, and to herself, that supernatural creatures, in particular vampires, didn't terrify her. The problem was, this one looked furious.

# CHAPTER 2

Tall—lofty was a better word—he filled the entrance with height and muscled bulk. Pale skin peeked through gaps between his gloved hands and his shirtsleeves, and around the covered portions of his face. He wore a wide-brimmed cowboy hat over dark-brown hair tied back in a medium-length tail. Sunglasses hid his eyes, and a bandanna covered his mouth and nose. Dressed in a dark-green shirt and jeans, he sported bright-blue cowboy boots and looked as if he'd just popped in from a rodeo. His long legs covered the distance in four easy strides, and he arrived at the counter with an air of frenetic energy around him—an energy that spoke of barely suppressed rage.

"You Kelsey Davis?" he asked.

She swallowed. How would a vampire she'd never met know her name?

He gave her no chance to respond. "You're the owner of this place, right?"

She set her spray bottle and rag down on the shelf under the counter and straightened her back, stretching to her full five-foot-five-inch height—for what it was worth. He dwarfed her, and she estimated he stood at least six-foot-five.

"Who wants to know?" Thankfully, her voice didn't squeak and betray her terror. She clutched her hands together in front of her to keep them from shaking.

"Your son is Joshua Davis?"

The terror broke free then, and without thinking, she raced around the counter, fists clenched. "What have you done to my son?"

He deflated a little then and rocked back on his heels. The furrows on his pasty-white brows smoothed out, and he yanked the bandanna from his mouth to reveal full red lips and a flash of white teeth. She could see no fangs in evidence, but then, wouldn't they only appear when he wanted to feed?

"What about my son?" Her voice remained high, and her fists were still bunched. She couldn't control them. It took all her self-control not to pummel him, and she raised her arms as if preparing to attack.

"Not about what I did to him. It's about what he's done with my daughter."

Kelsey's shoulders dropped, and she blinked and stared at him. "What?"

For the first time, he paused long enough to look around and notice their audience. The group of teens had stopped their exuberant chatter, Laura's nose no longer stuck in the book she held, and Chase stood behind the counter with his mouth hinged open.

The vampire stuffed the bandanna into the front pocket of his jeans and slowly removed his sunglasses. His deep brown eyes mesmerized Kelsey, awareness of her surroundings disappearing so that only he existed.

He cursed and slid the glasses back on to break the

spell. "Do you have somewhere we can talk in private?"

She shook off whatever traces of dopiness remained and told Chase to look after things. When he assured her he'd be fine, she waved a hand toward the back of the store. "Follow me."

She led the vampire into the staff room at the back of the bookstore, through a door displaying a sign that said *Employees Only*. The door thunked closed behind them, shutting them into a small space made even smaller by the vampire's looming presence.

Kelsey moved deeper into the room to give him space, dodging around the table and chairs she and her staff used during their breaks. Her gaze darted from his face to his body and back to his face. At least he kept the sunglasses on and wouldn't hypnotize her.

"Who are you? Why are you asking about my son? Why are you so angry?"

"Not angry at you. If that's the impression I gave, my apologies." His right hand made a move toward his face as though he wanted to remove the glasses again, but at the last moment, it dropped once more to dangle at his side. "Your son called me and left a distressing voicemail. I'm here to follow up."

"What did he say?" Kelsey couldn't hide the shock and fear in her tone. Why would Josh call this vampire? What could he possibly want with a vampire? A sudden horror that her son wanted this creature to turn him weakened her legs and almost had her dropping in a swoon. She locked her knees and brushed aside the insane thoughts.

"He was searching for my daughter."

"Your—" *The dhampir girl.* "Do you mean Dakota?"

"I do." He made that move to take off his glasses

10

again, but once more kept his hands away from his face. "Where's your son? I must talk to him."

*You and me both.* "Before you walked in, I'd have said he's at his father's. Did you try calling him back?" Josh had just turned eighteen, had his own cell phone and a part-time job. That he didn't work for her was a sore spot between them, but he'd explained he wanted to work in something related to archaeology, the field he wanted to go into. He'd gotten himself a job at the museum downtown. She understood how that helped him, but she'd looked forward to having her son work for her before he went off to university.

"Yes, I tried calling him back." Exasperation oozed from every word. His lips curved down, and she glimpsed eyebrow movement behind the glasses. His smooth, white forehead wrinkled to complete the frown.

"What did his message say?"

"That my daughter might be in trouble. Now, I know nothing about your son, and I know even less about you, so I called Annabelle." Kelsey threw him a quizzical look, so he said, "Dakota's mother."

"And?" she prompted when he fell silent.

"She says everything's fine."

Kelsey sighed in frustration. "Then why would Josh tell you it's not?"

"That's why I'm here." He leaned toward her. "When I asked to speak with Dakota, Annabelle said she wasn't available." He tilted his chin up. "I can't get my daughter on her phone. Something your son said has me worried."

"What?"

"He claims Dakota had to get away from home before her mother sold her."

# CHAPTER 3

Kelsey pulled the cell phone from the holster at her hip and called Josh, all the while keeping a close eye on the vampire. As she waited for her son to pick up, she said, "What did Josh mean?" She didn't even know how to phrase what she wanted to ask. What kind of mother would sell her child? Sell her to whom?

"He didn't go into detail."

"What's your name?"

"Philip Belanger."

That explained the slight accent—he had French in his ancestry. Did he originate from Francia or from Kébec? If the former, he could be centuries old, perhaps even from before the magickals revealed themselves to the mundane world.

A click in her ear signaled voicemail kicking in, and Kelsey had to leave a message for Josh to call her back. As she disconnected the call, she asked, "How'd my son know to call you?"

"Dakota must've told him about me." He tilted his

head to one side and studied her through his dark glasses. "They must be close friends for her to reveal something so personal."

Kelsey frowned and barely kept the distaste off her face. Dakota seemed nice enough, and Kelsey had never minded Josh talking to the girl, but after today, he should keep his distance. Better make sure he was where he should be. She opened her contacts list and placed a call to Blair. In answer to Philip's unasked question, she said, "I'll try my ex."

"Kelsey. What can I do ya for?"

She cringed. The split from Blair had been amicable—mostly—but she'd initiated it, and much of his habits and expressions now grated on her nerves. None of that was his fault, but it showed just how wide the chasm between them had grown by the time she'd called it quits.

"Is Josh with you?"

"No. I thought he was at the store with you."

She heaved a sigh. "Why would you think that? It's your weekend to have him." Hating to have this discussion in front of a stranger—a vampire, no less—she threw a miserable glance at Philip. His lips remained neutral, but for all she knew, his eyes were closed behind those shades.

"He told me you needed him this weekend, so I thought he was with you."

"Needed him for what? He doesn't work for me. You didn't think to confirm it with me?"

"No. Why would he lie?"

Kelsey paced the room in frustration. "Clearly, he did."

When Blair replied, his voice betrayed more frustration than concern. "He's probably kicking it up with his friends. I'll call him."

She remained silent, letting the dead air hang.

Finally, he said, "I'll track him down."

This time, the instant he stopped talking, she responded. "Don't bother. I'll do it. As always."

She hated how snarky she sounded. Perhaps this mess with Josh was karma getting her back for judging Dakota's mother. But the woman had slept with a vampire. Revulsion warred with contempt, and Kelsey flung another glance Philip's way. As she did, he made another move to remove his glasses, and this time, they came off.

She turned her back on him, then reconsidered as she realized she'd turned her back on a vampire. When she faced him again, she kept her gaze averted from his. Maybe he'd seduced Dakota's mother with that vampire stare. She couldn't imagine the woman had chosen to sleep with him. Rapists. That's what these creatures were.

Blair's voice wrenched her back to their conversation. "You know, Kelse, you always act like I'm a shitty parent. You're not exactly mother of the year yourself."

"What the hell's that supposed to mean?"

"Know what your problem is?" He gave her no opportunity to respond. "You think you're better than everyone. No one's as smart or as capable as you. No one's good enough for you. Or for your precious Josh. But you know who's not perfect? That's right—you."

"He's your precious Josh too. Isn't he?" She shook her head, though he'd never see the gesture. "You know what? I don't care what you mean by that. If you hear from our son, call me. I'll see what I can do at my end. He might have taken off with a … a girl." She couldn't tell her ex Josh might be with a vampire girl, even if she was only half vampire. Could dhampirs turn humans? Or was that only a power true vampires held?

Kelsey ended the call, her heart pumping rapidly with the fear that Josh had run away with this girl. Her shallow breaths punctuated the silence that followed, and involuntarily, she tilted her face up to meet Philip's gaze.

"I can smell your fear."

"Yeah, you and every other creature in this place." She scowled, but as she gazed into his eyes, she couldn't pull away no matter how hard she strained to do it. Gradually, her expression smoothed. She lost the desire to break the connection, and floated in his energy and power. A yearning to have him bite her neck had her tilting her chin higher.

He closed his eyes, shook his head, and massaged his temples. The connection between them snapped, leaving Kelsey panting with unwanted desire.

"I take it you refer to the pup I saw sitting in the café?"

She flushed, ashamed of her urges and embarrassed she'd insulted Laura. She'd meant only to insult him. Referring to magickals as creatures was politically incorrect, and, typically, she avoided it. But the more she associated with these non-humans, the more her inherent prejudices spilled out. They had no souls, and her interactions with both Laura and Philip today showed she judged them for it. It galled her to think that her ex could be right about her. He had to be wrong. From now on, she'd do better. Be better.

"I'm sorry."

"You don't get out much, do you?" He sounded amused now, and that grated.

"I get out just fine." She retrieved her purse from her locker. "I have to find Josh."

He took a step toward her. "I have to find Dakota. We can search together."

She flinched and sucked in a breath. "No. I doubt they're together." She lied about that. She was positive they were together, but no way in hell would she get into a car with a vampire.

"I won't harm you." He smirked at her. "I have no desire to turn you or seduce you."

Something about the way he said that last sent a wave of regret through her. She frowned. "Terrific."

"Your scent is savory rather than sweet. I have a sweet tooth." He mocked her; she was sure of it.

She glared at him. Whether she liked it or not, she didn't know where to start the search. She could use Philip's help if the places they needed to look were places Dakota would frequent.

"Where did you want to go?"

"First?" He licked his lips, a slow, lascivious gesture that had her quivering. "We'll visit Dakota's mother. She has some explaining to do." He smiled, but it wasn't meant for Kelsey, and when it broadened to a toothy grin, chills raced up her spine.

# CHAPTER 4

Annabelle Lawson lived near the crossroads where Kelsey had her café, but not near enough to walk there in less than a half hour. After informing Chase that she had personal business to attend to and asking him to close up the store if she didn't return in time, Kelsey retrieved her bicycle from the garage. She walked it around to the front where Philip waited.

His shades covered his eyes once more, and the bandanna was back in place. He wore gloves, and the only skin that peeked out was his forehead and the bit between his eyebrows just above the bandanna hooked over his nose. The brim of the cowboy hat offered shade and further protection to his face. Although the May day was overcast, it remained bright enough to cause pain to any part of him not protected. Kelsey assumed he'd slathered his face with sunscreen as well.

*Must be awful to always avoid the sun.* She couldn't imagine it. Though she made sure not to overexpose herself to the sun's rays, she loved the feel of sunshine on her skin when she stepped outside on gloriously bright days.

As soon as Philip laid eyes on the bike, he laughed. "What's that for?"

"What do you think it's for?"

"Darling, no offense, but I can be to Annabelle's and back before you're halfway there on that contraption."

She glared at him. "I'm not getting in a vehicle with you, and I'm not your darling."

"Don't take everything so personally. I call everyone I get the urge to snack on darling." He held out his hand. "I left the car at home. I can carry you."

"The hell you can!" She stared at his hand until he dropped it to his side.

"To save time, I suggest you take me up on this offer to transport you. Otherwise, you can wait here, and I'll tell you what I learn from Annabelle when I return."

"No. I need to go." Worry etched her features, and tears sprang to her eyes. What if something had happened to Josh? *And Dakota*, she reminded herself. She didn't wish any harm to the dhampir girl. Unless the girl had harmed Josh.

"Then for the love of God, put the bike away and come along."

"What do you know about God?"

"Probably as much as you know—perhaps more," he replied smoothly. His voice changed timbre, softening to the point where she sensed kindness. "You needn't fear me. I'm not dangerous to you or any human. Even if no protection laws existed, I wouldn't hunt you. I've lived off animal and donated blood for much longer than these laws have been in place."

"Easy enough for you to say. You hypnotized me."

"Not deliberately, darling."

"And you said you wanted to snack on me."

"I'm just being honest with you." He held out his hand once more. "Come. We don't have time to argue or to discuss theology."

"Discuss theology?"

"God."

*Oh.* She capitulated, not because she'd lost her fear of him, but because what he said made sense. They needed to find the kids.

"Wait here." She turned her back on him, an itch of vulnerability creeping up her spine the entire time she was in his line of sight, and wheeled the bike down the laneway to the garage.

When she returned, he held out his hand once more, and this time, she took it. He drew her to him and hoisted her into his arms. Inadvertently, she put her arms around his neck, and by the time she realized she was hugging him, he was already setting her on her feet again. Breathless from the rush across streets and sidewalks—had he flown?—she stumbled, and he steadied her with a firm hand on her upper arm.

She caught her breath. "How?"

"Not flying, if that's what you're wondering. It's more like moving at the speed of thought."

"All right." She made a mental note to research this when she had some time. If she ever had the time.

They stood now in front of a row of townhouses with tiny yards and exteriors in need of fresh paint. Garages reached the road, so the homes didn't even have driveways. Annabelle's house had a row of flowers along a walkway leading to two concrete steps. Kelsey couldn't see through the narrow window beside the front door, and the garage was shut tight.

"You think she's home?"

"I know she is."

Kelsey didn't want to ask how he knew. She hoped he'd called ahead, but maybe he could smell the woman through the walls. If that was the case, she'd rather not know.

He moved ahead of her to the front door and rang the doorbell. She strained her ears for the sound of footsteps and heard nothing. They waited. Somewhere, wind chimes tinkled in the light breeze, and she caught a whiff of lilacs. She searched for the source and found it at the house on their left. The lilac bush made up almost the entire yard. It smelled nice, but grew disproportionate in scale to the tiny lot.

Philip rang the doorbell once more, and both stared expectantly at the door.

"You sure she's here?" Kelsey asked, despite the risk of learning the reason behind his certainty.

"I hear her. Or someone."

For some reason, that eased Kelsey's mind. Acute hearing made him seem less animalistic than acute olfaction.

"You didn't phone her?"

"That would've risked her taking off to avoid seeing me."

"Why would she want to do that?"

"She wants nothing to do with me." He said it matter-of-factly.

"That doesn't bother you?"

"Why would it?" His tone and the way he angled his face at her made her think he was genuinely puzzled at her question and interested in the answer.

"You had a child together."

He sighed. "We did. Wasn't my doing."

*This creature—vampire—is so weird.* Why wouldn't she think him less than human if his every utterance reminded her he was … not human? She had a sudden desire to ask him about how it all happened, but since it was none of her business, she left it alone.

He lifted his hand to ring again when the door opened. A man stood in the entrance. As soon as he laid eyes on Philip, he tried to slam shut the door. The vampire stopped the man with a shove hard enough to snap the door from his grasp and bounce it off the wall. The man backed away and tried to run, but in a flash, Philip gripped the guy's throat with one hand.

"Where's Annabelle?" The vampire snarled, and his fangs sprang out.

A wet stain spread across the front of the man's jeans, and he thrashed and gagged. His lips, surrounded by thick, reddish-brown hair, parted, but only drool escaped his mouth.

"Let him go." Kelsey's voice cracked. What if Philip killed the guy?

Philip dropped the man, who landed on his ass on the tiled foyer floor. He scrambled to his feet and backed against the wall beside the coat closet. His long brown hair was mussed and tangled, and he clung to the wall as if it offered solace.

A woman's voice interrupted. "What's going on here?"

*Annabelle Lawson?*

# CHAPTER 5

Stumped for words, Kelsey allowed Philip to take the lead. He yanked the bandanna from his lips, letting it rest under his chin. He also removed his glasses, stared into the woman's eyes, and answered the question of her identity.

"Annabelle." He tossed a glance back at Kelsey. "Shut the door and lock it, darling. You're letting the flies in."

She did as she was told, unaware she'd done it until she found herself flipping the deadbolt to the locked position. Kelsey focused her gaze on Annabelle while sneaking the odd glance at the man leaning against the closet door. The faint odor of urine wafted from his pants.

"Who's the guy?" Philip asked, his expression impassive.

A tall, slim woman with cascades of black hair and deep olive skin, Annabelle wore a silk blouse and a denim mini skirt. She waved slender, ring-covered fingers in the unknown man's direction. "No one you need worry about. Change your pants, Marshall. I can smell you from here."

Before the man could move, Philip, his gaze fixed on Annabelle, said, "Stay, Marshall. No one leaves my sight until you tell me where Dakota went and what this guy's doing here."

Annabelle gave an exaggerated sigh. "Didn't I say he's not your concern?" She stared pointedly at Kelsey and said, "I didn't ask about your chippy, did I? You back on humans?"

"He's my concern if he's responsible for my daughter's disappearance—or if he goes anywhere near my daughter when she's here."

She laughed in his face. "What are you getting at?"

The vampire ignored the mocking laugh and stuck to what concerned him most. "Where's Dakota? If I have to ask you again—"

"You'll do nothing." She arched her shapely brows and half-turned as if she intended to walk away.

Philip snagged her arm, and she tottered on her four-inch heels, almost falling into him. She raised her hand, and for a moment, Kelsey thought the woman meant to slap his face. Instead, her eyes glazed over as her gaze met the vampire's stare. She licked her lips and then parted them.

"Philip." Her voice came out low and sexy.

Kelsey glared, but as soon as she realized what she was doing, she tamped down the surge of jealousy and relaxed her facial muscles. What difference did it make to her what these two did? She'd only met Philip today and didn't even like him. His vampire abilities had her insides knotted and her brain muddled. That's all it was.

"Well?" No one wondered "well what?" They all

understood what he wanted.

"She's not here," Annabelle murmured.

"Where is she?"

"Marshall helped her find a new home." Her words hinted at wistfulness, but no regrets.

"What have you done?" Philip's expression changed instantly to rage.

Kelsey finally found her tongue and broke into the discussion. "Where's Josh?"

When Philip turned his gaze to Kelsey, it broke the spell, and Annabelle visibly tensed in his grip.

"Who's Josh?" she asked, a slight sneer on her lips.

"My son." Kelsey kept her voice calm—no reason to yell and scream. If she remained polite, perhaps Dakota's mother would tell her where Josh had gone, and she could leave Philip here to sort things out regarding his daughter. This really was none of Kelsey's business. All she wanted was to locate her own child. "He's friends with Dakota. He's looking for her. Did he come here?"

"Oh, yes, the boy. He was here. Dakota wasn't, so he left when I told him so."

"Where'd he go?"

She shrugged, and when she remained silent, the vampire gazed into her eyes again and repeated Kelsey's question.

"Vampiretown," Annabelle replied, her voice soft, her eyes dreamy. "He went to find Philip."

Kelsey gasped and turned a fear-filled gaze on the vampire. "You didn't say he went to see you."

"He didn't," Philip said—no hesitation, and he sounded genuine.

Kelsey grabbed for the deadbolt, twisted it open, and jerked on the doorknob. "I have to find him. He's in Vampiretown. I told him never to go there. Why would he go there?"

"Kelsey." Philip's voice, low and calm, compelled her to freeze.

She dropped her hand to her side. "I have to find him."

"We'll find him. That'll be our next stop. He probably went to my place when he couldn't reach me by phone." He turned back to Annabelle, capturing her once more in his hypnotic gaze. "Where's her new home?"

"Marshall found her a place. Somewhere."

"Where?" he asked sharply.

"Well, I-I don't know."

Philip released her and grabbed Marshall once more, yanking him away from the closet door with a grip on his T-shirt. Kelsey heard cloth tearing, and Marshall cried out.

"What did you do?" Philip snarled at the man.

"Only what she asked me to do." He turned a pleading gaze onto Annabelle, but she shook her head at him and motioned for him to stay silent.

"What did she ask you to do?"

"Whatever it was," Kelsey cut in, "she doesn't want you to know. She's signaling him to keep his mouth shut."

"You bitch!" Annabelle snapped out. She took a step in Kelsey's direction, her jaw clenched and her face red.

Philip whipped out his free hand and grabbed her by the lapel of her blouse. "That's enough." He turned his attention back to Marshall. "Tell me where my daughter is or you can tell the cops."

"You think the cops'll care about a half-vampire

chick? She ran away."

As Kelsey wondered why Philip didn't just hypnotize the man to learn what he'd done, Philip did just that. He moved his grip to Marshall's face, squeezing his cheeks and forcing his chin up so their gazes locked.

"Where's Dakota?"

The man didn't hesitate as he fell under the vampire's spell. "We sold her. The slave market has her. She was auctioned off already."

An icy finger of revulsion traced its way through Kelsey's stomach, and she was afraid she'd throw up right there in the foyer.

Philip didn't so much as glance her way, but she knew he spoke to her when he said, "Get out of here, now."

The certainty that he would kill the couple if she left kept her rooted to the spot.

Philip angled his head so their eyes met, and the sense of melting into him grew inside her.

"Go." He then gave her instructions, his voice soothing and kind.

Kelsey opened the door and walked outside.

# CHAPTER 6

The stroll back to the café refreshed her, though as Kelsey walked, she puzzled over why she was outside. She had work to do at the store. Josh popped into her mind then, and along with that came a sense of unease. She took her phone from her purse and called him.

*Voicemail.*

"Where are you?" Something vaguely familiar about this call percolated at the back of her mind, but she couldn't retrieve it.

*Déjà vu.* That's all it was. Josh was at his father's right now. She considered calling Blair to ask him how Josh was doing but decided her son would resent her checking up on him. He'd reached that age where he interpreted everything his mother said or did as interference. After asking him to call her back, she disconnected the call and continued her stroll.

*What am I doing here?* She went for a walk every day—at least, whenever it was nice out—but she always went during her lunch break, and she wouldn't walk into this neighborhood. The homes in this section of the city were run-down, shabby. Most had peeling paint and weed-covered lawns. Retaining walls crumbled; hedges grew wild and untrimmed. Barbeques sat on driveways in front of garage doors. Many places had residents and neighbors, beers in hand and sitting on lawn chairs, clustered on front porches or inside open garages. She couldn't help staring and caught the eye of the odd person as he or she glanced over to see who walked past. Most looked friendly enough.

She'd become distracted again. What train of thought had she been following? Kelsey spun around to check out what she'd left behind. Where had she come from? She headed back to the café, that was certain, but she couldn't remember walking to wherever she returned from. Wouldn't she have had a destination? Even on a stroll, she usually had an endpoint in mind at the start of the outing. She liked to do a nice, long walk for the fresh air—such as it was in downtown Tkaronto—and always set a target. Uneasy, she realized she couldn't remember leaving the store.

Her cell phone, which she still held in her hand, showed the time was 4:40 p.m., which meant Chase was at the café. At least she hadn't left it unattended.

*Of course I didn't. Why would I even think that?* Because here she was walking down a street she never walked on, at a time when she never left the store, and returning from a destination she didn't remember. For a terrifying moment, she thought she'd had a stroke or had lost her mind. But that didn't track either because she, after doing a quick internal scan, felt fine.

The path she followed took her to the entrance of a small park. If she cut through it, she'd save time and reach her shop by five o'clock. Even this late in the afternoon the place was packed. Children played in the playground, though not as many as would've been there immediately after school let out. Parents, nannies, and other guardians watched over them. Others, out having a stroll or cutting through on their way to or from whatever they needed to do, hurried past Kelsey without a second glance.

She entered the park and inhaled the fresh air, imagining the oxygen released by the trees filling her lungs. A sudden feeling of buoyancy put a bounce in her step, and she smiled at a group of children playing hide-and-seek among the cluster of trees to her right. Colorful tulips, crocuses, and hyacinths grew in the carefully tended gardens on either side of the path. What a great idea she'd had to walk this way after all. Perhaps this had been her destination all along. She must have walked a circuit from the store just to cut through here.

Up ahead she spotted an empty bench among the trees. An urge to sit on it drew her over, and she settled down to watch the children play. Sunshine had warmed the wood, and now it warmed her as well, drawing a sense of peace and well-being through her. When her phone vibrated in her hand, she stared down at it as if surprised it existed.

*Why is my phone out? Oh, right*, she thought. *To check the time, of course.* Wasn't she supposed to get back to the store? The phone buzzed again, and she glanced at the call display. *Blair?* Why was he calling her? *Josh! What if something's happened to Josh?* The thought darkened the brightness of the day. She accepted the call.

"Blair?"

"Did you find him?"

Her heart skipped a beat. Did he mean Josh? Who else could he mean? "Who?"

"You're kidding, right?"

"What? What are you talking about?"

"I'm talking about our son. Have you found him? I've tried his cell twice and think maybe you were right to be concerned."

"I was?" She frowned. Had they talked today? She couldn't remember. Maybe she *had* lost her mind. Or had a stroke.

"Quit screwing around. Did you find him or not?"

At least she could answer that question with confidence. "No. The last time I tried his cell, it went to voicemail."

"Shit. Have you tried calling his friends?"

"His friends?" Something about that question brought that niggling sensation to the back of her mind again. "His friends come to the café." And hadn't she seen them all before she came out? A hazy memory of talking to one of the guys in that group grew less fuzzy as she focused on it. They weren't exactly Josh's friends—not his close friends—but he hung out with them when he visited the store and they happened to be there.

"Yes, his friends. What the fuck is wrong with you? Josh told me he would be at your place, and you said he's not there. Does that ring a bell?"

Suddenly, it rang a huge bell, loud and discordant, and Kelsey leaped to her feet. What was she doing sitting in the park when her son was missing? But was Josh at the store now? Perhaps he'd shown up while she was wandering around. "Yes. I'll … I'll see if his friends know and call you back."

"Are you okay? You don't sound right."

"Yes. I have to go. I'll call you later." She disconnected without waiting for a response. He'd understand. She'd return to the store and Josh would be there and everything would be fine.

She shoved her phone into her purse and returned to the path at a run. If she had to, she'd run all the way. Oh, why had she even left the café, especially if Josh was missing? She should've called the police already. Or not. There had to be a good reason for not calling them. Right?

Before she'd trotted even a mile along the path, she stopped short. A vampire blocked her way. He wore a cowboy hat. A bandanna covered his mouth and nose. His dark clothing covered every part of him except bits and pieces of skin she glimpsed around the bandanna and the dark glasses.

He removed the glasses. "I'm sorry I had to do that to you."

All her memories of the afternoon came crashing back, and fists flying, she attacked him.

# CHAPTER 7

Philip snatched the flailing woman into a tight embrace. With her arms out of commission, Kelsey used her legs. Under cover of his bandanna, he couldn't help but smile. While he was sorry he'd had to do what he'd done to her, her anger, to him, was more cute than dangerous. She reminded him of a raging bunny.

After letting her vent for a few moments, during which he caught a few invectives as well as a couple of well-placed kicks to the shin, he brought his mouth level with her ear and whispered, "Let it go."

She struggled for a second or two longer, and then, likely seeing the futility of what she did, collapsed against him. "My son. You made me forget about Josh." Her tone was accusatory and hurt, which was understandable.

"Temporarily," he replied.

She tried to pull away from him, but, afraid she'd attack him again and not willing to take the time to let her, he said, "Settle down. I'll help you find him."

To demonstrate his physical superiority, since she appeared to forget his superhuman abilities, he threw her over his shoulder, and in a flash, set her down again at the entrance to her café.

Kelsey whirled on him and slapped his face. It didn't hurt, since she was weak and the bandanna covered the cheek she'd struck; even so, he gripped the offending hand's wrist until she winced in pain.

"You done?" he snapped.

Tears rolled down her cheeks, and she shoved his shoulder with her free hand. "Leave me alone."

"Where's your home?"

When a look of fear crossed her face, he said, "Do you want to talk about this at your place of business? Where do you live?" He heaved a frustrated sigh. "If I wanted to hurt you, I'd have already done it."

"Unless you want to get me alone where you can murder me." Her expression turned to horror. "Did you murder Annabelle and her boyfriend?"

Now his eyes widened and his lips pulled back in fury, but she'd have had difficulty recognizing the rage under the glasses and the mask. When he spoke, though, his tone made it clear. "No, and I resent your accusation." He shrugged. "Besides, if I'd killed them, I wouldn't have left any witnesses."

She shuddered at what his words implied but refused to let the subject drop. "Which is what you might be attempting now. You sent me away. You forced me away. Now you want to get me alone. What else would I think?"

"I needed to talk to the mother of my child in private."

"Did you hurt them?"

Before he could respond, the entrance door

opened, and Chase stepped out. "Everything all right, Ms. Davis? This guy bothering you?"

She took a moment to respond, but when she did, she said, "I'm fine. Can you close tonight by yourself? I have to take care of some personal things."

"Sure." He threw a suspicion-laden glance at Philip before settling his gaze on Kelsey. "You'll call if you need anything?" His tone broadcasted his certainty that she'd need rescue from the vampire.

"Thank you, Chase," she said. "I'll be fine."

He gave her a nod and went back inside, letting the door swing closed behind him.

Kelsey walked down the sidewalk leading away from the café's entrance but hung a left when she reached the end of the red-brick building.

"We'll go in through the back." She led the way into the alley between her store and the restaurant next to it.

"You live here?" Philip made small talk to distract her. "You own it all?"

"Yes to both."

"What made you open a business at the crossroads?"

She paused in her stride. "That's personal." She resumed walking.

A breeze blew through the alley, sending her dark-blonde hair swirling about her elfin face. Maybe she had elvish blood in her. That would explain her vivid blue eyes and delicate build, but he knew that wasn't the case. The lapel pin she wore identified her as pure human, and a mundane one at that. She had not a trace of psychic ability nor any other paranormal talent some humans possessed.

They reached a gate and she opened it, letting them

into a postage-stamp-sized backyard. Flowers and a stone path wound from one end of the yard to the other, forking at one point to lead to the back door of the building. She followed that trail and dug into her purse for her keys, which gave him an opportunity to scope out and appreciate the vegetation growing throughout the garden. Most of the plants were in the ground while others overflowed a variety of pots. A small pond with a tiny waterfall made the focal point of the yard. A gazebo, lush grass surrounding it on all sides, stood in the far corner.

"I see you enjoy gardening."

She led him up a set of iron stairs to the second level and unlocked and opened the steel door at the top. "Yes, but it's tiny. I don't get to flex my green thumb too much. I'm grateful for having it though." She hesitated before saying, "Do I need to invite you in?"

He chuckled. "If that were a thing, Marshall could've shut the door in my face. You seem to know the myths better than the facts, darling. That tidbit was likely created to make humans feel safe—as if they had some control over vamp home invasions. If I want in, your lack of permission won't keep me out."

To prove it, he brushed past her into a small foyer fronting a galley kitchen on his right and a living-dining room combo on his left. Beyond that, a hallway lead to what he assumed were bedrooms and bathrooms. The decor was simple but elegant, and more than one surface held a vase of flowers, which gave the room a slightly cloying smell. He wasn't opposed to the fragrance—it simply overwhelmed his sensitive olfactory sense.

At least the flowers almost overpowered the scent of her blood. While he wasn't in any danger of attacking her and draining her, he'd found her scent made him salivate from the moment they'd met. He hated to admit it, even to himself, but she attracted him at a visceral level.

"Okay, we're alone." She planted her feet, crossed her arms, and blocked his exit from the foyer. "Shut the door."

If this was how she wanted to play it, he'd humor her. He eased the door closed, and, just to watch her jump, locked it with a loud twist of the deadbolt. But her look of fright changed instantly to worry.

"My primary concern is my son." She paused. "And your daughter. We know she's in danger. What did they tell you after you kicked me out? Josh is probably further along in tracking her than we are. If we find him, we might find her."

"I searched the house, focused on her room. She doesn't have her cell phone with her." *Because you don't sell a teenage girl to slavers with her cell phone on her.* Philip snarled as he yanked the bandanna down from his face. "Her room was neat and clean—as if she never even used it."

Kelsey's face brightened. "But Josh should have his cell on him. We can track him." She uncrossed her arms and spun on her heel.

He followed her into the living area where she had a small desk set up near the door he assumed linked the apartment with the store. While she waited for the machine to boot up, she gave him a shy, sideways glance.

"Would you like something to drink?"

He smiled at her sudden interest in playing hostess, as if she'd just remembered her manners. It amused him. She amused him.

"Thank you, no." As it was, he had to keep his distance from her. When he drew within a foot of her, her scent was so strong he could almost taste her, and he was sure she wouldn't allow him a sample.

"They said Josh went to Vampiretown." She logged into her computer.

He tried to ease her worry. "They don't attack humans anymore—at least, most of them don't."

"It's not the gentle, law-abiding majority that concerns me," she said.

"Have you ever been to Vampiretown?" Even as he asked, he knew what she'd say.

She shook her head.

"In your whole life? Never curious as a teen?"

"No. So what?"

He laughed.

"What's so funny?" She frowned.

"No need to get defensive. Tell me why you bought a store at the Crossroads when you so clearly fear hypernaturals."

"I don't fear them." She turned her full attention to the monitor and used her mouse to open a browser. She tilted her head down, and her hair curtained around her face.

When he smiled in amusement again, she didn't notice.

"You'll think it's stupid."

He contemplated the statement. "You needn't worry about what I think."

She tucked her hair behind her ears and entered Josh's phone number into the locater app. "I wanted to get out and experience new people, new things. I'd never been out of downtown Tkaronto. I grew up there, married; we bought a house there, and we raised

Josh there."

"Until your divorce."

"Until our divorce."

"Why would that be stupid?"

"Because what you said is true: I *am* afraid of hypernaturals. I never knew any when I was growing up—or even after. Your kind doesn't tend to buy homes in human-populated subdivisions."

"Yet humans buy outside their clusters." He'd always believed that a strange phenomenon. Humans had even bought in Vampiretown. No law against it existed—anyone could buy wherever they wanted—but most wanted to buy where others like them settled. He could understand sticking to your own kind. He sometimes ventured out of Vampiretown, but he never wanted to move out. Living surrounded by your own kind brought comfort and reassurance, even if you didn't get too chummy with others. Vampires leaned toward self-isolation, and Philip preferred living alone and keeping to himself, as most vamps did.

Kelsey broke into his thoughts. "Found him." She tilted her head up to meet Philip's shaded gaze. "He's in Vampiretown, just as Annabelle said."

"I'll take you," Philip replied. "Make sure you have a photo of your son we can show."

"On my phone."

They left the building through the back, avoiding Chase and anyone who might be in the café.

# CHAPTER 8

Vampiretown sprawled across the area west of the Crossroads. Kelsey insisted they take her car—she refused to have the vampire carry her again. In her mind, she'd ceased calling him by name ever since he'd sent her away from Annabelle's. He'd used hypnosis, or something similar, to influence her mind and control what she did. He'd made her forget her mission to find her son.

As they drove along the highway leading into Vampiretown, she asked him why.

"I needed you out of there."

"That's not an answer. Why did you want me out of there?"

"I said 'need' not 'want.' "

"I heard. Didn't agree with the need."

She watched for the signs directing her to Misizaagiing, the official name of Vampiretown. According to the GPS locater on Josh's phone, she had to take the second exit and first head south and then west. Josh, for whatever reason, had gone to the heart of downtown Vampiretown—and that was if he still had his phone. She didn't want to dwell on the possibility he'd lost it, but the thought popped into her head whenever a lull hit the conversation.

"What happened with my daughter is personal. It's none of your business what goes on between her mother and me."

"It's my business if it affects my son, and it definitely affects my son." She gripped the steering wheel tight and her teeth gritted.

"My relationship with her doesn't. Besides, I couldn't leave you alone with them while I searched the house."

"Why?"

"The less they know about you, the better, darling."

"I'm not your darling." But her tone lacked conviction this time—not that she wanted him to think of her as darling; she was just too exhausted to quibble about it.

Her phone buzzed and she answered it using the hands-free option. "Hello?"

"Kelsey? Did you reach Josh?" Blair asked.

"I tracked his cell. I'm heading out to where he is now."

"Where's that?"

"With his friends, I guess. A restaurant." She wasn't sure why she didn't want to reveal Josh had gone to a bar in Vampiretown. Who was she protecting? Josh? He knew he wasn't allowed to visit hypernatural colonies alone and without permission.

"All right. Let me know when you have him. We'll have to ground him, you know."

"Of course I know." She hadn't meant to snap at him, but she resented his implication that she wouldn't properly discipline their son. "Call you later." She disconnected the call.

"Why'd you lie to him?"

"You know how your relationship with Annabelle is none of my business?"

"Just making conversation. You don't have to bite my head off." He laughed at the joke while she glared at the road ahead.

Despite a reluctance to involve the vampire in her personal life, she answered the question anyway, more out of a need to talk it through with someone, anyone, rather than bottle it up. "Blair doesn't need to know. If I tell him, he might go racing out there."

"You mean like you are?"

"What do you expect me to do? I have to find my son. Plus, I know your daughter's missing and …" She trailed off when it occurred to her she didn't know where they could start the search for Dakota. Josh's presence in Vampiretown meant he hadn't found the girl—Kelsey was sure of it. Where do you sell a dhampir girl? Not in Vampiretown! That could get you killed, especially if the slavers were human. Trying to broach the subject tactfully, she said, "Did Annabelle tell you where they left Dakota?"

"She did."

When he didn't elaborate, Kelsey prodded. "And?"

"When we locate your son, I'll see what he can tell me and hunt them down."

"Did you hypnotize Marshall to get the information?"

"Had to. He wasn't willing to rat them out. They paid for her." He spat that last bit out in disgust.

"We have to report them to the police."

"I'm sorry, darling, but you must forgive my

reluctance to deal with the human system."

"The vampire department, then. We're headed right there."

"Dakota's a dhampir. They won't care either."

"Why? What makes you think they won't? Police do their jobs because they want to help people."

"Your naiveté is sweet. Don't ever change."

Stuck without a retort, she found her exit and drove onto the off-ramp in silence.

Traffic slowed to a crawl, and Kelsey focused on the road as clouds rolled in and threatened rain.

*Great.* She tried to recall if the weather report had indicated a storm, but she remembered she hadn't checked today. Why would she? She hadn't planned to go out.

"Do you know where this bar is?" He could at least help her navigate through the downtown corridor. "What are all these cars doing here? Don't most vamps travel the way you do?"

"Sure. These'll be tourists—humans and others coming out here to partake of the wilder side of life, if you know what I mean."

"No, I really don't."

"How old are you?"

"None of your business." The most oft-repeated phrase between them. Would they ever build enough of a relationship that they could ask one another personal questions without restraint?

"You have a teenage son, you use some kind of elixir to erase the fine lines and wrinkles, and you dye your hair, probably to hide some gray strands. I assume you're middle-aged. Forty or so. Am I right?"

*Forty-three*, she replied silently. "None of your business." How'd he know about the elixir? She sometimes felt guilty for using a magick potion to make herself look younger, but it wasn't damning magick if it was made from herbs and boosted with only a light spell. Surely God wouldn't hold that against her. She bought the mass-produced elixirs from the store, not from a mage or witch. Everyone over forty used them. She suddenly had a flashback to shouting at Josh when he wanted to do something just because his friends did it—the old jumping off the bridge to follow the crowd rebuttal. She scowled at Philip.

"No need to get offended. It's just a number. Whatever it is, it's far less than mine."

She threw him a venomous glare. "You look twenty-five. What do you care about age?"

"My maker turned me when I was forty-five. Whatever my physical appearance, I'd matured first. Since then, I've lived and learned even more."

Kelsey sighed. "Sometimes I'd love to look twenty-five forever. I looked pretty good then."

"You look pretty good now. Smell all right."

Her eyes widened in horror. "Smell? You ... I ... like what?" She gulped.

"No need to panic. I smell all you humans— hypernaturals too, if you want to get specific. Anything that pumps blood."

"So ... not vampires?"

"No, but I sense vamps in other ways."

She was afraid to ask, but curiosity forced it out of her. "In what ways?"

"They have an aura."

"You mean light?"

"Not exactly. I sense the energy they emanate."

She tried to sense any energy he might emanate and felt nothing. A psychic friend had once referred to

Kelsey as dead inside. The remark wounded her even though she knew her friend hadn't meant to offend. The truth was, Kelsey hadn't any intuition at all. She never had gut feelings, never sensed things that weren't there. She assumed haunted houses would appear to her as regular houses, but she preferred not to test that particular hypothesis.

The bar loomed ahead on the right, and she pulled the car into the parking lot. Since it was packed, she drove around until she located a free spot close to the road but far from the building. When she cut the engine, she moved to get out, but the vampire stopped her.

"Not you."

"Oh, yes, me."

"Must you argue about everything?"

"Must you? We're searching for my son. I'm going in. You can't stop me."

"Sure I can."

When he made a motion to take his shades off, she grabbed his arm. "Don't even think about it."

He shook off her hand, slipped the bandanna from his mouth, and removed the sunglasses. "I wasn't going to hypnotize you. You want to come in, we'll set some ground rules."

She huffed and crossed her arms. "Such as?"

"You stay by my side. Always. Got it?"

Without meeting his direct gaze, she glared at his mouth through squinted eyes. "My son's in there." *Maybe.* She preferred to ignore the other possibilities.

"Unless you agree to stay by my side, you're not going in there."

"Why?"

"Have you ever been in a vampire bar?"

"You know I haven't."

"Then you agree to stick to my side the entire time we're in there. You need to use the bathroom, I go in with you."

Her jaw dropped. "Are you joking?"

His expression told her he was serious. *Dead serious.* Inside, she chuckled at her little joke.

"They'll swarm you, darling. Every one of them. Unless you're with another vamp."

"They wouldn't hurt me, would they?"

"Probably not."

"Oh, God, Josh is in there, maybe alone. I have to go." She threw open the car door and leaped out.

The vampire rounded the car in a flash and blocked her way. "Promise me you won't leave my side unless I say so."

"All right. Quit grinding on it."

"Promise."

"I promise."

"And I do the talking."

Kelsey stifled a sob. "All right. Please, I have to get in there."

He took her arm. "Let's go."

# CHAPTER 9

Bartenders at Blood Shots Vampire Bar didn't limit themselves to serving shots of blood, but the name horrified, and at the same time fascinated, Kelsey. Her eyes grew ever wider the nearer they drew to the entrance. The vampire kept one hand on her arm, and she found it reassuring enough that she didn't complain. The automatic door slid open as they stepped close to the motion sensor monitoring the entrance, and darkness and noise spilled out. Anyone they met gave the vampire a respectful greeting and stepped aside to let them pass. No one tried to stamp their hands or bar their way. Maybe Philip was some kind of VIP there.

*Figures he'd be a regular.*

The aroma of incense and cigarette smoke, beer, and fried food slammed her nostrils as they crossed the foyer into the bar. The decor was early sex-addicted crazy person. Leather covered everything, and whips and chains hung from the ceiling and accented the walls. Red lights splashed everything with a bloody glow.

*Josh is here?* The thought of it made her want to throw up. When she got her hands on him, she'd let him have an ample piece of her mind. Wait until she told Blair where she'd found their son! Yes, Josh was going to hear about it, but first, she would sweep him into her arms and cry and hug him and thank God for keeping him safe.

*Please, God, keep him safe.* She slid her hand under the neck of her blouse and fingered the chain around her throat. A small gold cross hung from it. She refused to pull it out here, but it eased her fear when she thought of it or touched it.

The vampire guided her around writhing bodies—both human and hypernatural. As she dodged around a gyrating troll, she wondered why he was considered "hyper" natural. By definition, the term implied some kind of enhancement that made him more than human. As far as she could see, trolls looked similar to humans, had no magic, and weren't magic, but they were abnormally strong. The one she saw here was short, squat, and had skin the color and texture of granite.

They weren't human—she agreed on that front—but extra human? Extra ugly, sure. Extra dimwitted, yes. What was this one doing out among people, anyway? Trolls hated people. Yet here was one that gave lie to that belief. He grinned at her, showing a mouthful of crooked razor teeth, but he didn't seem nasty.

She glanced toward the windows high above the entrance—the only way to tell if it was day or night other than to check the time. Trolls turned to stone when exposed to sunlight, and perhaps that marked them as hypernatural. The sun had set only recently, so he likely hadn't been here long.

The troll danced with a pixie so tiny that the monster had to hold her in his upturned palm so he wouldn't inadvertently step on her and crush her. Her gossamer wings fluttered in time to the throbbing music, and she wiggled her tiny ass. Somewhere nearby, hooves pounded the floor. Kelsey searched until she located the centaur. He held a stein of ale and sipped from it as he danced with his partner, a human woman.

A pause in the vampire's stride yanked her from her gawking.

"Backroom. Through there." He pointed toward a closed door on the other side of the bar.

"You know the owner?"

He either ignored the question or didn't hear her over the din. Likely he ignored her since vampires had keen senses all around.

She let him lead her to the door, which had a sign on it declaring it private. He didn't knock, but turned the knob and walked right in as if he belonged there.

Compared to the rest of the bar, the office sported a rough elegance. A teak desk dominated the room, which was lit by wall sconces. The walls were painted moss green with rich mahogany trim. A vampire sat in the leather desk chair, and when he looked up to see who'd intruded so rudely on his work, his expression of irritation turned to delight.

"Philip. What are you doing here? I thought you weren't coming in until tonight." He stared hungrily at Kelsey and, to her horror, parted his lips, baring his fangs and running his tongue lasciviously over his front teeth. "Got yourself a human?"

"No, he—" she attempted, but Philip silenced her

with a tug on her arm and a stony glare.

"I need information, Dwayne."

"Sure. You want the computer?"

"Probably." He guided Kelsey to the leather sofa at the side of the room and sat her on it. She gave him a dirty look, but he'd already turned his back on her and moved to one of the two leather armchairs in front of the desk. "I'm searching for a boy who might've come in here recently. He'd be underage, so I suspect the bouncer told him to move on. Except the GPS on his cell phone still pings to this location."

Dwayne frowned. "I didn't get any report of an underage kid crashing the party."

"He's searching for my daughter."

"Here?"

"Likely suspected she might come here seeking my help."

Kelsey processed the tidbits she gleaned from the conversation. Philip was part owner of this orgy palace? His comment that the bouncer would've ejected Josh both relieved and concerned her. If Josh had left, why did the GPS on his phone indicate otherwise? Dwayne clearly knew of Dakota's existence, but he hadn't admitted he'd seen her at all.

"You got a picture of the kid?"

Both vampires turned to stare at Kelsey.

She rose, phone in hand, and strode to the desk. After calling up a recent picture of Josh, she passed the device to Dwayne. As he took it, their hands brushed against each other, and his tongue darted from his mouth again to lick his lips. He inhaled deeply before leaning over the cell phone to study the picture.

"Didn't see him myself." He sat up, his back straight, and leveled a gaze at Kelsey. "Doesn't mean he wasn't here." He pressed a button on the landline sitting on his desk and spoke into the intercom. "Thrasher? Get someone to cover the entrance and come back to the office." He released the button and said, "Thrasher was the bouncer on duty. Started in the afternoon, so if the kid was here before that, we'll have to ask Cruncher."

"Thank you." She didn't know what else to say. Josh had come into this place, and a vampire named Thrasher or Cruncher had confronted him.

A rap on the door announced the bouncer's arrival, and when Dwayne called out for him to enter, the door opened, and a gargantuan outhouse of a man entered, ducking under the door frame. Kelsey had assumed they'd have vampires covering the entrance here, but she'd been mistaken.

Thrasher's lapel pin, if not his size, identified him as a giant. Made sense. Who'd argue with a guy ten-feet tall and as wide as two burly men fused together? His muscles bulged even when he wasn't flexing, and he showed them off in a gigantic tank top that probably could've covered an actual tank.

"Yo! What you need, boss?" He looked from one employer to the other and settled on Dwayne. "You call me?"

"Yeah." He asked Kelsey to show the bouncer the photo, and when she held the phone out, the giant palmed it in his turkey-sized fist. "Look closely and tell the lady if you saw this kid here today."

Thrasher glanced at the picture, then did a double-take of recognition. "Yeah, he was here. I told him to leave."

"Did you see him leave?"

The giant shrugged. "I thought he did. He didn't get

into the bar. Not past me, uh-uh."

"But did you see him leave?" Dwayne persisted.

"Not exactly. He left through the front entrance. Where he went after that, I can't tell you. It's always busy, and I had to watch who came in, not who walked away."

Kelsey threw a worried glance at Philip. "Then why is his phone still here, and how do we locate it?"

"Call it," Dwayne replied.

"I've been calling it all afternoon," she said. But she retrieved her phone from the giant and called Josh's cell.

"Put it on speaker," Philip instructed, and she did.

Philip opened the office door and listened. When he appeared to catch what he sought, he stepped from the room. He shouted to Kelsey as he walked away. "Stay with Dwayne."

She gave Dwayne an uncertain glance and hurried after her vampire.

# CHAPTER 10

Philip picked out the ringtone from Josh's cell as it echoed after the ring from Kelsey's phone. The sound came not from the bar's lounge but from the washroom area. He burst into the room and tracked the sound to a spot behind a trash can. He plucked the phone off the floor and spun around to face Kelsey as she pushed her way into the room.

"I told you to wait with Dwayne."

"No, you told me not to leave your side."

"Unless I said otherwise. I trust Dwayne to keep an eye on you."

He'd no sooner spoken than Dwayne pushed through the door. "You can't wander around here unaccompanied," he told Kelsey.

"I don't care about that." She spun around and confronted Philip. "You found Josh's phone." She held out her hand, and he passed it to her. "Where is he?" It came out a wail.

"We'll find out." He waved at the door. "Now, let all these gentlemen piss in private, darling, and step outside."

She gaped at the row of urinals and stalls, her face flushing as awareness of their location dawned on her.

Almost every unit had an occupant. At least the stalls had doors, but the urinals gave her an eyeful. She rushed from the room, and Philip and Dwayne followed close behind her.

Irritated he had to babysit this human, which slowed his search for Dakota, Philip took Kelsey's arm and directed her back to the office. Dwayne returned to his seat at the desk. Thrasher had left, probably back to his station at the front entrance. More roughly than necessary, Philip shoved Kelsey onto the couch.

"Stay there. Give me your phone, and I'll ask around if anyone saw Josh in here. Someone must have seen him."

"I'm coming with you."

Philip ignored her—no time to argue or explain. "Keep her here," he said to Dwayne.

"You owe me," his partner replied as Kelsey leaped to her feet and yelled, "No way."

"Deal." Philip breezed from the room. Behind him, the ruckus began. It made him grin.

\*\*\*

Kelsey struggled against the vampire holding her captive, but her attempts to shake him off were futile. Dwayne didn't bother to argue or reason with her. He simply held her in a tight embrace until she tired of the effort.

"All right. I'll sit down and wait," she shouted. He released her, and she dropped onto the sofa, glaring at him all the while. "Why do you care if I leave this room?"

"He cares, so I care," Dwayne said.

"Why?"

Dwayne returned to his seat behind the desk. When she glanced at the door, he said, "You'll never make it, and if I find it helpful to tie you to a chair, I'll do it."

"Is your business so dangerous I can't walk into the bar by myself?" She genuinely wanted to understand.

"You don't know what you're doing, and we don't need a lawsuit against this bar if some vamp grabs you and taps your veins or some hypernatural sexually assaults you. You come here on your own, you'll sign the waiver when you enter, and whatever happens is all on you." He turned his attention to the monitor in front of him and went back to working on whatever they'd interrupted when they'd first walked in.

She fell silent, mulling over what he'd told her. After a few minutes, she spoke again, unable to dampen her curiosity. "Have you and Philip owned this place for long?"

Dwayne raised his face from the monitor. "You want a coffee while we wait? Looks like with you here, I won't get much work done."

Her hopes rose at the thought he'd leave her alone, but then she realized she wouldn't leave anyway. At some point, she'd resigned herself to wait here in safety and trust that if Josh was in the bar, Philip would find him.

"No, thank you."

"All right." He leaned back in his chair. "To answer your question, we've owned this place since the unmasquing."

"You were both alive then?" That made them … she did some calculations … at least a hundred years old. If Philip had turned when he was forty-five, he was at least 145 years old.

"We were both turned before that time." He opened a drawer in his desk and pulled out a pack of cigarettes. "Mind if I smoke?"

"Kinda, yeah."

He dropped them back in and sighed. "Ah, well, I can wait."

"Vampires can get addicted to cigarettes?"

"Not addicted, love, they just don't cause us any harm. Nothing can harm you if you're already dead." His eyes, which she noticed now were a light hazel, twinkled as he met her gaze. She tried not to look directly into them in case he wanted to hypnotize her.

"The bar was filled with cigarette smoke."

"More than just cigarettes."

"Is that legal?"

He laughed. "You haven't visited Vampiretown before, have you?"

"No." She scowled, annoyed that these vampires treated her like a virginal young girl. Here she was about to start menopause any time now, and they acted as if she were some kind of neophyte. Yet when it came to hypernaturals, she was.

She made a mental note to do some research into the various cultures. Even if she had no direct experience with them, she could see how understanding her customers would be useful. She should've done this before she'd bought her store. Except if she'd known what dealing with these creatures was like, she might never have taken that step.

Dwayne rose from his seat and went to the wet bar she hadn't noticed tucked into a corner behind a pillar at the other end of the room. "Drink?"

"No, thanks." No way would she cloud her judgment with alcohol in this place. "What was it like? Before the unmasquing?" She'd heard there'd been a time when humans and hypernaturals battled for supremacy. Millions had died. She was lucky she'd been born long after the wars had ended.

"Sometimes I think we should've stayed hidden, but the pandemic pushed us out into the open." He poured whiskey into a crystal glass, raised it in *salud*, and sipped.

Kelsey had studied the pandemic in school, but hearing about it from someone who'd lived through it made it more real. "Did you want to unmasque?"

He shrugged and returned to sit at his desk. "Truthfully, I didn't care one way or the other. At the time, we thought the vampires would win, and we'd raise humans for food."

She blanched and he noticed.

"Nothing personal. As you can see, we don't attack you on sight anymore. We don't even hypnotize you to trick you into giving it away."

"Because it's illegal and you'd be charged."

He laughed again. "Law or no law, if I wanted to suck your blood, I could do it, and you wouldn't remember it'd happened. The marks would fade quickly, and no one would be any wiser."

"So you're an upstanding citizen. What's in it for you? For vampires?"

"Peace. No one hunts us, but we still satisfy our hunger."

"You don't mind drinking donated blood?"

"Plenty of humans enjoy allowing me a taste. It's a delightful kink for some people. Donated blood is still blood though. Tastes the same regardless of the source."

"Does it?"

He grinned. "Some tastes sweeter." He sniffed the air. "You're more savory, I'd guess. More bloody mary than caramel syrup."

That shut her mouth and kept it shut for another few minutes. She was just about to ask him another question when the door banged open, and Josh stumbled into the room, followed closely by Philip.

"Found him, darling," the vampire said.

"I'm sorry, Mom," Josh blurted simultaneously.

# CHAPTER 11

Before anyone else reacted, Kelsey gave a squeal and leaped from the couch. With a choked sob, she hurled herself at Josh and threw her arms around him.

"Oh, God, you're safe. Thank God." She pulled away and held him out at arm's length.

He scowled. "Mom, let me go. It's fine."

She ignored him and, with a critical eye, examined him from head to toe. He appeared unharmed. When he tried to shrug off her grip, she said, "Hold still. You've got some explaining to do, but I want to make sure you're okay first."

Did his eyes look tired? Had a vampire hypnotized him? She brushed his hair back from his ears, despite the swats he took at her hands, and examined his neck.

"He's unharmed. No one fed on him," Philip said.

A choked cry escaped from her at the thought that someone could have done just that, but she believed the vampire's claim that no one had touched him.

"Where were you?" She spoke to Josh, but turned

her questioning gaze to the vampire.

"I found him creeping around the private rooms."

Afraid to ask what went on in the private rooms, but needing to know what her son had been up to, with a waver in her voice, she asked, "What was he doing?"

"Peeking." For the first time, Philip's face betrayed a hint of rage. "The security team will hear about this." He pointed an accusing finger at Josh. "You'll tell them everything you did to sneak in here and avoid detection."

Josh looked sheepish. "Yes, sir. If it helps, it wasn't easy. I think I lost my phone somewhere along the way, too." He looked at Kelsey, meeting her gaze with confidence and a lack of remorse. "I'd do it again. I'm sorry I worried you, but my friend is missing. No one seems to care."

Quickly, because it appeared Philip took that comment personally, Kelsey replied, "Her father cares. I care. You should've come to us before you searched here for her yourself. You also lied to your father." She gave him time to let that all sink in and waited to hear what he had to say.

His cockiness eased up, and he had the decency to look remorseful this time. "Dad knows?"

"He knows you're not at the store with me, and he's worried about you too."

"What will you tell him?"

"Nothing." When he looked relieved, she said, "I'm not telling him. You are."

"But, Mom—"

She cut him off with a wave of her hand and a stern expression, and looked from Philip to Dwayne. "Thank you, both, for all your help." She returned her gaze to Philip. "If you need our help to search for

Dakota, please let us know what we can do. At this point, I think you need to report this to the police."

He made no comment on her suggestion about the police but said, "Please stay long enough for me to debrief Josh with my head of security."

She agreed, and Philip called his head of security to the office. The vampire who showed up was female and dressed like a sexy cop, but she took her job seriously. She questioned Josh for over an hour, and by the time she finished, Kelsey was sure no one would ever sneak into this bar again.

When the security officer completed her interview, Philip escorted Kelsey and Josh out, but this time, he led them through the back way rather than through the packed bar. He hadn't put the bandanna back in place, nor did he wear his sunglasses. No need. Night had deepened, which cast the parking lot in a bloody glow from the neon signs on and around the bar.

They arrived at Kelsey's car, and she told Josh to get in and wait for her. She tossed him the keys so he could start the vehicle and listen to music. When he was safely tucked into the front passenger seat, she returned his cell phone to him with a curt "We'll talk about this later." She slammed the car door shut with more force than she'd wanted. Even though he'd done this out of concern for his friend, he'd put himself at risk, and that continued to infuriate her.

"Go easy on him," Philip said, correctly interpreting her mood. "He meant well. I'm touched he cares so much about my daughter."

Could vampires feel touched? She didn't know, and right now, she didn't care. "Don't worry. He'll survive my wrath. But he has to understand he can't do something this risky without consulting us."

"He probably weighed the options and decided asking forgiveness was preferable to asking permission." He stepped to the car's passenger side. "I didn't bring this up inside, but I need to ask him what he learned about Dakota."

"Of course." She tapped on the window, and Josh opened it.

Music blasted out, and he turned it off, giving them a puzzled look.

"What did you find out about Dakota?" she asked. When he hesitated and gazed uncertainly from one adult to the other, she said, "Her father wants to know. He's worried about her."

"Well ..." Josh pressed his lips together.

"Josh! Tell him what you know." She could imagine what Philip must be going through—she'd gone through it herself when she couldn't find Josh—but Philip's agony must be much worse. If she'd learned traffickers had her son, she'd be far more panicked and upset than the vampire appeared.

"I didn't find her."

"Clearly," Philip said. "What did you find?"

"That she's not here."

The vampire scowled and crouched down to put his face level with Josh's. Kelsey immediately yanked on his shoulder in an attempt to prevent him from hypnotizing her son. Philip was immovable, but when she tugged on him again, he whirled around and snarled at her. "Leave me be."

She took an involuntary step backward, but he closed the distance between them in one stride.

"I won't let you hypnotize him." But she didn't know how to stop him if that's what he intended.

Josh flung the car door open and leaped to Kelsey's

defense. He threw himself, fists raised, between his mother and the vampire.

Philip laughed. "Try it, boy."

Kelsey touched a hand to each of Josh's shoulders. "He won't hurt me." Her voice held more assurance than she felt.

"It's fine, Mom. I'll take care of it." Her boy, who sounded more like a man just then, lowered his fists. "I'll tell you what you want to know. You really want to find Dakota?"

"Yes." The vampire, head tilted to one side, lips pursed, studied the young man before him. "Did you doubt that?"

"She never met you."

"How did you know where to find me?"

"She knew about you, who you are, but she said she'd never met you." His tone was accusatory.

"Not my decision."

"Not hers, either."

"Why did she tell you about me?" Philip stepped away from them and leaned against the car, arms folded, feet crossed at the ankles—the picture of nonchalance.

Kelsey eased out from behind Josh and positioned herself away from, but halfway between, the two males: one human, one monster. She focused on each speaker, trying to read body language and catch nuances of expression and tone. She'd never been good at sensing people's moods or determining if someone lied, but she had to try.

"We talked on the phone sometimes," Josh said.

Kelsey frowned. This was news to her. She didn't expect to know everything about her son, but she'd thought she knew who all his friends were. She'd considered the dhampir girl an acquaintance—someone Josh chatted with sometimes when she came to the store with her friends. Kelsey had, until now, paid so little attention to Dakota she hadn't even bothered to notice the girl wasn't human.

"She confided in you?" Philip asked.

"Some. She was scared of her mother, of Marshall." Josh threw Kelsey a quick, uncertain glance, but when he spoke, his voice was firm and confident. "Marshall is a dick."

"Agreed. But you haven't answered my question. Why were you searching for my daughter here? Did she tell you she planned to visit the bar?" Philip's brow furrowed.

"She said she contacted you, and you told her to meet you here."

The astonishment that crossed the vampire's face couldn't possibly be fake. Kelsey was sure if the car hadn't held him up, he might have fallen over.

"I never spoke to her." He pressed a palm to his face for a moment, and when he lowered his hand and met Josh's gaze again, his eyes flashed dark and deadly in the dim light. "When was this meeting to take place?"

"A half-hour before I called you. I planned to be her backup in case things went sideways. We wanted to meet here fifteen minutes early, and I'd hide and watch you guys talk. She never showed, and I couldn't get hold of her on her cell. I thought maybe she went to your house instead, so I called you. You know the rest."

"She never called me. What made her think she'd reached me?"

Josh closed his eyes, as though trying to visualize

what had happened. "She called the bar. Told them she wanted to talk to you. They put her through, but she got your voicemail. You—or someone pretending to be you—returned the call." He fell silent and became lost in thought for so long that Kelsey wondered if he'd finished all he had to say.

Just as she opened her mouth to suggest they head home, he spoke again, his gaze fixed on the vampire. "She believed she spoke to you and that you'd protect her. So she wanted to come here. I convinced her to let me watch from a distance in case … in case it was a trap," he finished, his eyes apologetic.

"Are you sure she never showed?"

Josh shook his head. "Either that, or I missed her. One thing I know for sure: she's gone and someone took her."

Kelsey and the vampire exchanged glances. Her son didn't realize how close to the truth he'd veered, and she didn't know if they should tell him.

# CHAPTER 12

By the time Kelsey parked the car in the garage and escorted Josh up the back stairs and into the apartment, she was exhausted and ready for bed even though it was only nine o'clock. She tossed her purse onto the couch and decided she was more hungry than tired.

"Josh?" She could hear him thumping around in his room and wondered if he'd forgiven her for what he considered abandoning his friend.

As they drove home, he'd grudgingly called Blair to apologize for the lie he'd told, accepting it as the right thing to do. But he only told his father he'd been tracking down a missing friend and left out most of the details. She kept her thoughts on the ethics of disclosure to herself, however. She still had Josh's anger and resentment to deal with. Kelsey's insistence they leave the hunt for Dakota to her father and the police—whichever division he planned to call—infuriated Josh, and his attitude and arguments against it made it clear.

The problem was, the vampire hadn't promised he'd call the police. She supposed if the traffickers who took the girl were human, he could deal with them, but the idea of him going vigilante didn't sit well with her. However, she wasn't bothered enough to interfere. The child wasn't hers. This wasn't her business. All the decisions related to Dakota's welfare were up to her father and her mother. Was it Kelsey's fault one was a worse monster than the other? Wasn't Dakota herself half monster?

As Kelsey entered the kitchen, she called out to Josh again. "Josh? You hungry? I'll throw together some snacks."

Her son had accused her of callousness, which hurt. He'd insisted they should get involved, should help search for Dakota, even if it put their own safety at risk and despite Philip's insistence he didn't want their help, wouldn't appreciate their help, and wouldn't save their interfering hides if they got into trouble helping him. Philip still refused to reveal what he'd learned from Annabelle and Marshall after he'd sent Kelsey away, and she agreed it was better that way.

From the fridge, Kelsey took out a package of cheddar cheese, a loaf of salami imported from Magyarország, sweet green peppers, olives, tomatoes, a loaf of rye bread, and the butter. She munched as she put together a platter for herself and Josh. This simple spread was solid fare that would ease the hunger pangs nicely. She carried the platter into the living room, along with two plates.

Perhaps she'd pour herself a glass of wine and watch some television while she ate. She and Josh could bond over one of his action movies. She always preferred the weekends when he was here with her, even when he didn't hang out with her but went with his friends, and didn't mind that she'd have him all to herself tonight. Tomorrow, of course, would be a different story. Since they hadn't told Blair everything that had happened, they'd have to have that conversation with him when he arrived to pick up Josh. She pushed thoughts of how that might play out from her head. Time enough to worry about it in the morning.

Silence from Josh's room drew her attention. He had to be hungry—she was sure he'd had nothing to eat while at the bar. Considering he was a teenage boy, he should've been out here rummaging through the pantry for food already.

"Josh?" She rose from the couch and walked toward his bedroom. When she called out again, she didn't shout in case he'd fallen asleep from exhaustion.

*Poor kid.* He was so worried about his friend.

"Hey, you awake?" She listened at his door, and when she heard nothing, turned the doorknob and stepped into the room.

\*\*\*

A two-story drop should've prevented Josh from climbing out his window, but thankfully, his mother had bought an emergency escape ladder to store in his room in case of fire. He appreciated her foresight, because Dakota's kidnapping constituted a serious emergency and justified his use of the ladder. His mother would freak out about it, and he didn't blame her, but she'd get over it when he returned with Dakota. His father would also get angry, but more because Mom would vent her anger to him than because Josh had left home. Dad would understand you had to protect your woman.

That Josh considered Dakota his woman without her knowing it was just a technicality. He'd intended to ask her to be his steady girlfriend, and he knew for sure she'd say yes. Just because she'd disappeared before they'd had the chance to formally cement the relationship meant nothing. She'd agree and they'd be a couple, ergo, she was his woman and he should protect her. Whenever he recalled how his mother had ordered him to stay out of it and let Dakota's father handle it, his determination to find the dhampir girl grew. How could his mother refuse to help? Couldn't she imagine what Dakota must be going through right now? They had to find her—fast. The longer it took, the lower the odds they'd find her at all.

He barely noticed the chilly night air as he slipped through the back gate and into the laneway behind the yard and the garage. Josh had a bike in the garage, but his mother had the remote to operate the garage door opener in the house. He'd have to walk. Josh also had his driver's license, but if he couldn't get to the remote, he certainly couldn't get to the car keys. Besides, he had his limits on what he was willing to do behind his mother's back. Stealing her car was one step too far over the line.

He wasn't sure where to head after the first stop he intended to make. His mother had known something more about Dakota's disappearance than she was letting on, but she refused to share the information with him. He'd have to puzzle things out on his own, like a detective. He grimaced. His mother treated him as if he were twelve. He was eighteen, for God's sake—almost a man. He might as well be a man, since he was the only male in the house.

Behind him, his mother's voice bellowed his name out into the silent night, and he winced. Christ, did she have to shout at him and alert the entire neighborhood to their personal business? As he hurried along the sidewalk—almost running now in case she got the car out to search for him—his phone vibrated in his pocket. He checked the call display, saw his mother's name, and declined the call. When she texted, he responded, because he wasn't a total asshole, but only to tell her to leave him alone, that he was visiting a friend. Her next step would be to track him via his cell phone, so his first stop was his buddy Anthony's house.

Anthony lived within walking distance, and Josh arrived a few minutes later. He rang the doorbell, and when his friend opened the door, Josh nudged him into the house.

"Dude, what are you doing? I was just about to head out to the party. Why aren't you already there?"

"Long story," Josh replied. "I want you to swap phones with me."

"Now?"

"I can't explain, but you have to be me and text my mom if she calls or texts. Just tell her you're at the party and will be back by midnight."

Anthony grimaced. "She's going to figure out our scam, and you'll get me in deep shit too."

"I didn't see you complaining when I pretended to be you so you could go to that concert your parents grounded you from attending."

Reluctantly, Anthony handed over his phone in exchange for Josh's. "Just don't do anything stupid, and if she threatens to come get you, I'm calling you, and you'll have to drop everything and get to the party."

"No problem."

"So … where ya going?"

"Can't get into that right now. I just need her to think I'm at that party. She's less likely to try to drag me from there. If she thinks that's where I went, she'll be pissed at me for leaving without telling her, but she'll be relieved I'm not doing what I'm planning to do."

"And what's that?" Anthony smirked. "Is it a girl? Doesn't your mom let you visit girls? What does she think you're gonna do?"

Josh hesitated. He didn't want to get into it all—it really was a long story—so he said, "Yeah, it's a girl. I need to track her down, and I don't want my mom tailing me." His expression turned serious. "This is important. You got this for me, right?"

Anthony nodded. "No problem. You owe me one, though—right?"

"A big one," Josh replied. *A very big one.*

# CHAPTER 13

Darkness always lightened Philip's mood, but this time, nightfall's charms were lost on him. No sooner had Kelsey's car disappeared from view than he rushed back into the bar to question his partner. Who else but Dwayne could possibly impersonate Philip? Who else had access to the phone in the office? Of course, by the time Philip reached the office, he'd arrived at more than one name. Even so, Dwayne remained the most likely suspect, and Philip meant to raise the issue immediately.

While Philip had never met his daughter, he'd kept tabs on her as she grew from the moment he learned Annabelle carried his child. Loathe to recall the night they'd slept together, which he considered the biggest mistake of his life—more a reflection of the mother than anything personal against the child—he realized he'd have to dredge it up eventually. Doing so would help fuel both his rage over what had happened and his determination to find Dakota. Anyone who harmed the girl would pay; he'd see to it personally.

He'd left Marshall and Annabelle alive, but that didn't mean he intended to allow what they'd done to go unpunished. Until he found Dakota, the couple could carry on believing they'd gotten away with it. Philip was patient.

But first things first. He burst into the office ready to torture his partner if Dwayne showed any hint of involvement with Dakota's disappearance.

It was empty.

Philip strode to stand behind the desk, and once there, studied the landline as if it held the secrets of the universe. Putting it on speaker, he checked the voicemail. The one new message was business related, so he waited for the saved messages to replay. No message from Dakota existed. If she'd called, whoever picked up the message had also deleted it. It made sense. If Philip had discovered it as a saved message, he'd have known someone else had listened to his messages. He'd also have phoned Dakota back.

He called Dwayne's cell.

"Dwayne Rathburn. That you, Belanger?"

"Who else would use this phone?" He said it jokingly, but he wasn't kidding.

"What's up?"

"Did you retrieve a message meant for me yesterday?"

Silence. Philip allowed it to drag on. Finally, Dwayne spoke. "Not to my recollection. Is there a note? I'd have saved the message and left you a note."

"No, but I know a message left for me was deleted."

"What's going on?"

"My daughter left me a voicemail message. I never received it." He didn't hide the accusation in his tone.

"You implying I had something to do with that?"

"I'm asking."

"Wasn't me. Any messages of yours I pick up, I pass along. If you'd had a message from your daughter, I'd have phoned your cell to let you know. I know how sensitive that issue is for you."

Philip frowned. He dropped into the chair behind the desk and tapped his fingers on the desktop. "Any idea if someone came into the office to use the phone? Or if someone accessed our voicemail?"

"Like who? Anyone uses this phone we know about. I haven't given out the password for the voicemail. Have you?"

He didn't reply. Didn't have to. They both knew Philip wouldn't have given out that kind of information. Which again left only Dwayne—or a hacker. Dwayne sounded sincere, and they'd been partners for over a century. Nothing serious had ever come between them in all those years.

*First time for everything.* "Fine. Thanks. I had to ask."

"Sure. I get it. Check the video cameras. Maybe they'll tell you who came into the office when we weren't around. Or get the tech guy to see if there's a way to retrieve the deleted message."

All were good suggestions and eased Philip's suspicions. After telling Dwayne he'd be focused on the search for his daughter, Philip asked his partner to come in early to run things in his absence. Dwayne agreed and they ended the call.

Philip accessed the video footage from the camera installed in the office. If the call had come in the previous day, he'd have to review everything from the time before he came in to work. By the time he arrived, the message was gone, because he always checked messages before starting his shift, and yesterday was no exception.

After more than an hour of trolling through video footage, he nailed down when the call came in by watching the LED on the phone and comparing arriving calls with the timestamps on calls that hadn't been deleted. Dakota's call appeared to come in at 1:15 in the afternoon. Philip had arrived at work yesterday at four o'clock. His evening had been uneventful. Nothing suspicious had happened—just all the regular weirdness of running a bar with a diverse and strange clientele.

None of the footage showed anyone other than Dwayne using the desk and the phone, so either Dwayne had deleted the message and lied about it or someone had hacked them. Unless Dakota had lied to Josh, which was a remote possibility, someone had retrieved the message, deleted it, and called Dakota pretending to be her father. Philip's hands fisted and he gave the top of his desk a right-handed thump.

Philip had enough doubt about Dwayne's involvement that he wouldn't question his partner again right now. That left checking out the video footage from the parking lot cameras to see if Dakota had made it to the bar at all today. At the same time, he could verify when Josh had shown up. From there, he could access traffic cameras and try to spot Dakota's car on the road between her home and the bar or her school and the bar. If someone had snatched her, it was likely along one of those routes.

*Marshall.* The man's name popped into Philip's head. Annabelle's boyfriend had arranged this, and he'd likely had the resources and knowledge of Dakota's personal life to trap her.

*Should've killed him when I had the chance.* Except it was

more important to keep him alive until Philip found Dakota. Then she could have the honor of putting the animal down.

Over a century and a half of life had provided Philip with skills, knowledge, experience, and contacts on which he could draw. A vampire friend worked in the vampire PD, and he had contacts in the police department serving the various human sectors, including the one where Annabelle lived. They'd get him access to the traffic-camera videos. Philip picked up the phone to make the calls.

\*\*\*

Darkness surrounded Dakota as well, but she welcomed it less than her father did. She could see well in the dark—more than a human could, but less than a vampire. She lay curled up on her side, wrists and ankles bound with zip ties, on a cot with a bare mattress and no blanket or pillow. Dakota assumed this meant her stay here was temporary.

They'd had a blindfold on her but removed it when they dropped her on the bed. At first, she feared they'd rape her, but after they dumped her here, they left and never returned. She didn't know how long she'd spent waiting for something to happen. It'd been long enough her terror had ebbed, allowing her to plan her escape. She had to do something before they came for her again—and they'd come for her; she was certain. You didn't kidnap people and then leave them in a room to starve to death.

It would be prudent to explore the room. Her captors might have a camera trained on her, and she weighed the pros and cons of sitting up and letting them know she was awake and aware. In the end, she decided it didn't matter to them, and pretending to sleep provided no advantage. They wouldn't expect her to be groggy because they hadn't drugged her when they forced her car off the road and dragged her into the back of their windowless van. Such a fucking cliché, but there you had it.

She hoped Josh had at least alerted someone that she was missing. He'd know when she hadn't shown up at the bar that something had gone wrong. They hadn't discussed that possibility, though, and she didn't know what he'd do.

Thinking of Josh brought tears to her eyes. She hadn't cried up to this point, not even out of frustration or fear, but she missed her friend. Boyfriend, maybe. She was sure he wanted to discuss their relationship with her.

He was so sweet. Even though they'd mature at different rates—technically, she was five, though in dhampir years she was eighteen like Josh—they could make it work. For the next eight years, she'd be on par biologically with her human counterparts. After that, she'd age one year for every ten years of life. Dhampirs weren't immortal the way vampires were. She'd die of old age in her dhampir-year eighties or nineties, but it would take her a long time to hit that milestone. Josh would die before her, and that was the one thing making her hesitate to get involved with him.

Sure, they were both young, and she understood intellectually that most would consider a first relationship temporary, but she loved Josh. Just because most first loves ended didn't mean theirs had to. They could be the exception. She had to get back to him.

*Get up. Help yourself. No one else will.*

She sat up, swinging her feet onto the floor, and scanned the room. She spotted the dark outline and hint of white porcelain that told her a toilet stood in one corner of the room. No sink stood next to it, so they didn't care if she washed her hands after. She wrinkled her nose in disgust. The room was empty of all else except the bed on which she sat. No evidence anywhere of a camera.

The door was directly across from the bed, and it looked solid. No window. No doorknob. She assumed it locked and opened with a key on the outside, perhaps a handle above the lock. She stood and closed her eyes for a moment, contemplating, recalling the information she'd studied about breaking out of zip ties. The moment she'd learned her mother planned to sell her, she'd read up on what to do if kidnapped. Dakota always liked to plan ahead, and no matter how surreal it was, no matter how unbelievable it was that her mother would sell her, she made plans for the eventuality she'd want to escape from whoever purchased her.

She positioned her elbows on either side of her torso, raised her arms, and smashed them down, bringing her elbows to each side of her waist. With that much force acting on them, the zip ties broke, and her hands were free. Next, she examined the bed frame for sharp corners, and when she located a solid edge underneath, she used it to cut the ties on her ankles.

Dakota quickly moved to the door and ran her fingers over the lock. Next, she removed a hairpin from her hair. Before she'd stumbled across her mother's plans, Dakota had never pinned her hair back. After, she kept several pins hidden in her hair and practiced picking locks with them. She unbent the pin, which she'd stripped of its plastic tip before putting it in her hair—no need to fuss with that under pressure. The tip was already slightly bent and perfect for the job at hand. Her hands shook slightly, so she had to slow her breathing and ground herself before she could continue.

The procedure didn't take long, and she heard the tumbler click. Since the door had no handle, she pushed on it, gently, and was relieved, though not surprised, when it nudged open. She gripped the edge of the door, allowing it to open only a crack, and listened.

Silence and a small glow of light greeted her. Opening the door wide enough to squeeze her slim frame through, Dakota slipped into the hallway. Now all she had to do was find an exit.

# CHAPTER 14

In the ten years Frank Evans had been head of the Tkaronto crime syndicate, he'd had many near misses and one direct hit that left him blind in his left eye. He wore a patch over it—no glass eye for him—and considered the overall effect roguish. Sometimes, when he wanted to terrify or repulse someone, he ripped off the black cloth covering and stared them down. Evans, mid-height, slender, black hair close-cropped, was human, but he preyed on the weak as well as any monster, and he was leader of his pack.

He lived north of the city on ten acres of farmland he rented out to a dairy farmer who also used the land to grow buckwheat, corn, and carrots. The people Evans dealt with in his various legal enterprises considered him a fair and reasonable businessman. His wife and children loved and respected him, and he loved and protected them in turn. But the men he shared his criminal activities with were his trusted family. Together, they'd built a small empire, and it ran beautifully. He loved the syndicate game: running guns and magickal weapons, dealing drugs and illegal potions, buying and selling slaves—men, women, and children of every species.

He'd fallen into it organically. His father, his grandfather, and his great-grandfather had all gone into medicine. His great-grandfather had been a surgeon, working his way up to chief of surgery in a, what was then, Toronto District Hospital. By the time Toronto became Tkaronto after the plague ended in 2025 and the magickals appeared, Evans's great-grandfather held the position of Minister of Health for Ontario. Skirmishes with the magickals had upended the entire system, and by the time the dust settled in 2075, his family no longer held power and was destitute. By the time Frank was born, his parents barely scraped by. But young Frank saw opportunity to fill needs for humans and magickals alike in the new system. That most of these unmet needs wandered into the realm of illegal activities or substances bothered him little. It meant he could charge more for whatever his customers wanted, and much of it was for drugs he could access from his family's old connections.

Though once upon a time he'd done it all for the money, the chicks, and the kicks, he now did it for the sheer energizing joy that came from having power. Evans owned politicians and cops as much as he owned properties and expensive toys. So when Sabatino, his second in command, buzzed Evans at home as he ate dinner with his family to tell him some kid looking for a dhampir girl they'd sold that day had visited the bar in Tkaronto, Evans made it clear he resented the intrusion.

"Why is this my problem?" Evans set his gold fork

down next to the slice of roast beef on the gold-trimmed china plate. He waved at Noleen, his wife, indicating she should continue eating. His two kids didn't need prompting; they ignored the interruption and ate in silence without glancing up.

"He tracked her to us," Sabatino replied. "It's not so much the kid that's the problem. He claims her father wants her found."

Evans's face darkened and he frowned. Lowering his voice, he said, "Who's the father?"

"Philip Belanger."

Evans rose from the table and strode from the room. Behind him, a maid who'd stood at attention by the dining room table as the family ate rattled cutlery as she cleared his plate. He made his way to his home office at the back of the house on the first floor.

"Why the fuck do we have Belanger's girl?"

"Her mother sold her to us. She gave us ownership papers and everything. We already had a buyer lined up, and they're delivering her in the morning."

"You knew she belonged to Belanger and you still bought her?" Evans and Philip Belanger had a civil business relationship. Evans agreed to leave the vampire and all that was his alone, and Philip agreed not to destroy all that Evans held dear.

"The mother said she didn't know who the father was. We only found out when the kid looking for her spilled the beans."

"Why wouldn't you do a DNA test?" But he knew the answer to that. They'd gotten sloppy over years of doing whatever the hell they wanted. Who'd expect a random dhampir girl from a nobody mother would be related in any way to Philip Belanger?

"We planned to. The mother hadn't done it, and the

81

girl was snapped up so quickly it didn't get done."

Evans fell silent, thinking, as he dropped onto the couch in his office. Finally, he said, "Get her back to him."

Now it was Sabatino's turn to let the silence drag on. When he spoke, the fear in his voice was evident. "We can't."

"Why? Tell them you'll find a replacement. One dhampir girl is the same as the next."

"Not to this buyer."

A chill speared up Evans's spine. His voice low and measured, he asked, "Who's the buyer?"

Sabatino told him.

Evans paled and flop sweat moistened the shirt on his back and under his arms. "Grab two guys and come out here to the house. We have to figure this out or we're all dead. Make sure you're not followed."

*\*\*\**

The hallway was lighter than Dakota's room, but not by much, and she considered it an advantage. Her captors were human. She'd smelled their blood when they'd taken her. If she could've used her fangs on them, she wouldn't be in this mess, but based on how things played out, they'd been prepared and experienced. They'd chained her with silver.

Rage bubbled up at the thought that others had gone through this, and Dakota vowed to get involved and do something about it the moment she escaped. Her dream had been to get into the computer industry as a game programmer, but she might reconsider. Perhaps fate had brought her here so she'd change her career path.

Shaking off the thoughts of vengeance before they got too distracting, Dakota crept down the hallway, but as she passed the first closed door, she froze. She pressed her ear against it and listened. She heard soft sobbing, and she smelled fear and blood—mermaid blood. Not only had this happened to other people, it was happening to them right now.

What should she do? If she stopped to unlock every door with a captive inside, she'd increase all their chances of getting caught. But if she escaped alone, by the time she returned with the police, anyone trapped here might be gone. Dakota made her choice, pulling her hairpin out again and crouching in front of the lock. She'd compromise and take one captive with her. They'd escape and lead the police back here. Then the cops could sort it all out and find the other victims. She hoped they'd beat it out of the bastards who'd done this to her.

She picked the lock on this door as quickly and expertly as she'd done the one on her room's door and pulled on the handle to swing it open. The cot on the other side of the room creaked as whoever was on it sat up and cried out in fright. She whimpered and pulled her knees to her chest, wrapping her arms around her shins.

"Shh!" Dakota hissed at the girl. "I'm not one of them."

The girl lowered her legs to the ground and stood up. Thankfully, mermaids had legs when on dry land, or rescuing her would've been an impossible task.

"Who are you?" the girl asked.

"No time for that. Come on. We've got to get out of here."

Without another word, Mermaid Girl hurried over

and the two joined hands as they slipped into the hallway.

Dakota estimated Mermaid Girl's age as younger than her own, but not by much. Even so, the girl huddled close to Dakota, leaning on her, letting her take charge. The mermaid's hand shook in Dakota's grasp, and it didn't stop there. Her whole body trembled, and Dakota heard the odd sob catch in the young woman's throat.

They descended the stairs as quickly as they dared, Dakota terrified of creaks that could alert their captors. So far the way seemed clear. The lack of lighting, while a good sign in Dakota's mind and not a problem for her, caused issues for Mermaid Girl. She stumbled more than once, and she held one arm out in front of her at all times to feel her way along.

They no sooner reached the bottom step when the lights flicked on and the click of a gun preparing to fire broke the silence.

"Freeze." The man's voice was gruff and angry. "The bullets in here are silver."

Both young women halted, and Dakota turned to face their captor.

# CHAPTER 15

Loud music and strobe lights greeted Philip when he arrived at Night Owls, the bar Frank Evans owned. Philip had traced his daughter's kidnappers to this location, and he seethed with rage at the thought that Evans had dared break the bargain keeping the peace between their worlds for so long. While Philip knew of Evans's illegal activities, he ignored them so long as Evans and his gang left Philip and anyone involved with him alone. They even went so far as to provide help to each other if needed, though Philip limited the assistance to strictly legal activities.

Once, Philip's own activities would've been more illegal than legal, but he'd slowly whittled those transactions down to nothing. For the past five years, everything he did was completely legit, but extricating himself from his former partners in crime, such as Evans, hadn't been completely clean or simple. The best he could do was forge an understanding to ignore what they did. Until now.

Yet he didn't want to burst in and demolish the place without giving Evans the chance to explain himself and undo the damage he'd done. Before he confronted the syndicate boss, he intended to verify he blamed the right crew. With luck, this was all a simple misunderstanding. They'd retrieve Dakota for him, and Philip would forget anything had ever happened—as long as they hadn't harmed her in any way.

He strode into the bar as though he owned the place. Instantly, he caught a whiff of fear and a familiar scent. He followed the trail to the offices at the back where he knew he'd find Josh Davis.

\*\*\*

Josh's plan to leave his phone with Anthony should've worked, and under any other circumstances, it would have. But these weren't any other circumstances, and he hadn't counted on the magnitude of Kelsey's fury at her son skipping out on her like that, nor on her fear that he'd disappear the way Dakota had. He'd gone to a party? Without her permission and telling her— telling her, not asking her—when he'd return.

She tracked his cell phone all right. She tracked it right to the party and refused to leave until they presented her with Josh or a reasonable facsimile. She'd put it just that way: "Get me Josh or a reasonable facsimile thereof."

It'd been an attempt at humor laced with sarcasm, but she hadn't expected they'd bring her the facsimile and not the genuine article. Yet here was Josh's friend Anthony standing in the doorway with the blast of music and light and raucous chatter spilling out from behind him. He reeked of beer and held out her son's cell phone while he begged her not to get mad at him.

"He asked me to do him a favor. I couldn't say no," the kid said.

She shook her head. "You sure could say no. It's easy. You just string 'n' and 'o' together and say 'no.' " She fisted her hands on her hips. "Where is he, Anthony?"

"Running an errand."

"What errand?"

The boy, same age as her son, tall and lanky and almost a man, pleaded with her with his eyes. He shrugged, holding his arms with hands palms out, the picture of innocence. "I don't know. He never said. Just told me he had to find someone." He averted his gaze and added, "A girl."

"And you've been texting me anytime I send Josh a message." She wasn't asking.

"Well, yeah. That was part of the favor."

It occurred to her then that Josh likely had Anthony's phone. "Have you talked to him or texted with him since he left?"

"No. Didn't need to."

"But I asked him questions." She couldn't believe what she was hearing. "You replied as if you—" She cursed under her breath, and the raised eyebrows on the kid told her it hadn't been as under her breath as she'd wanted. "Track your phone."

"What?"

"You heard me. Track your phone. I want to know where he went, so you're going to find him for me."

"He'll get mad at me."

She glared at him. "So will your parents if I call them right now and tell them what's going on."

He threw up his hands and clawed the air before

him in a placating gesture. "All right. Fine." He asked for Josh's phone and, after a few minutes, told her Josh was at a bar in downtown Tkaronto. "Night Owls."

"Thank you." She accepted Josh's phone back from his friend and turned on her heel. Before Anthony could disappear into the house, she peered at him over her shoulder. "I won't call your parents this time, Anthony, but this will never happen again. If it does, I'll find out because I'll check every time, and then I'll tell your parents. Understood?"

He nodded, a mixture of relief and deference on his face. "Understood."

She barely heard his reply. She was already down the steps and headed for her car.

\*\*\*

When Philip burst into the office where the thugs who'd discovered Josh skulking about Night Owls held him, he was never more relieved to see a vampire in his life. Josh understood this wouldn't end well for him with his mother—Philip would rat him out—but he'd at least live to see another day. Even better, they might reveal to the vampire information on Dakota they'd never reveal to a kid.

Gangster #1 and Gangster #2 both leaped to their feet the second the door swung open, and they raised guns they'd kept handy as if they expected trouble.

Gangster #1, a surly lard-ass who nevertheless moved with agility, confronted the interloper. "You can't be in here."

"I disagree," Philip said. "Where's my daughter?"

"We don't know nothin' about your daughter."

Josh had to hand it to the guy; he dared lie to a

vampire when all the thug had going for him was bullets and brawn. Using either would only enrage the hypernatural.

"You and your buddy here"—Philip gestured at Gangster #2—"ran her off the road and snatched her. You brought her here. Where is she?" He spoke calmly, but his tone sent a chill down Josh's spine. It had no effect on the thugs, because they continued to point their guns in Philip's direction, and the lunatic doing the talking continued to argue.

"She's not here. I don't know where she is. Sorry. We had a girl here. She's gone. Sold. We had nothing to do with it. We were just the middlemen, and no one mentioned she was yours."

"Why's the kid here?" Philip nodded at Josh.

"Social call."

The vampire snarled, and in a blink had both men by the throat, lifting them off their feet, one in each of his long, slender hands.

As their air supply dwindled, each man flailed his arms and kicked his feet. Both had dropped their guns. Josh remained frozen in his chair, unsure whether to pick up the weapons or run for the door.

"Evans. Where is he?"

Gangster #2, all skin and bones and expensive clothes, lost consciousness. Philip dropped him on the floor. The man landed with a thud, the back of his head hitting thin carpeting over hardwood. On his left wrist, he wore a watch Josh had seen advertised once for $5,000. He stared at the watch and, for a second, wondered if he had the nerve to steal it while no one was looking. Where had that idea come from? He shifted his gaze to Philip and Gangster #1, and Josh forgot all about the watch and his questionable ethics.

Gangster #1's face was beet red, and his mouth opened and closed as if he wanted to speak, but no sound came out. Philip tossed him onto the nearby couch.

"Where's Evans?"

The man gasped and wheezed, but couldn't form words. Philip waited. The man on the floor stirred, and when he sat up, Philip yanked him to his feet by his collar.

"Evans."

"Home."

Philip stared into the man's eyes, but Josh didn't think the vampire had mesmerized him. Gangster #2 didn't have that glazed look entranced humans got when vamps did their thing on them. Perhaps Philip avoided using his powers whenever mundane means would work. Was it a code of ethics this vampire followed, or did they all subscribe to that policy?

"Was that so hard?"

Gangster #2 shook his head so emphatically, he looked close to passing out again.

Philip released him, and the man staggered to the couch and dropped onto it.

In what was probably an effort at maintaining his tough-guy facade, Gangster #2 said, "Evans'll be pissed if you show up there."

Philip didn't spare the man another glance but turned his full attention on Josh, who swallowed his nerves and met the vampire's gaze head on. Before anyone could speak, a racket came from the hallway, and a woman's voice hollered, "Let me go. I can walk on my own."

*Oh, great.* His mother had arrived.

## CHAPTER 16

Déjà vu hit Kelsey as she stood in the doorway of the Night Owl's back office and stared at the group inside the room.

The bouncer who'd dragged her there released her arm. "She insisted on coming back here."

"You're holding my son," she retorted. "You're lucky I didn't call the police."

"Mom—" Josh started, but he was outshouted by Gangster #1, who hollered, "You're lucky we didn't call the cops, lady. He's trespassing."

She glanced from Josh to the thug, who looked as if he'd gone a couple of rounds with the vampire in the room. It made her smile. *Serves him right, if for nothing else than calling me "lady."* He may as well have ma'amed her.

"He's leaving. Now!" She sent Josh a steely glare. "Let's go."

"Mom—"

"Now, Josh. We'll talk about it outside."

Philip held a hand out to Josh, who ignored the offer of assistance, rolled his eyes, and got to his feet.

"I'll escort you out." The bouncer held the door open for them and waited as Josh joined his mother, who'd stepped back into the hallway.

Philip waved to the two goons. "You'd better hope I find Dakota tonight, or I'll be back." He followed Josh from the room.

The bouncer accompanied them from the bar. When they hit the parking lot, Philip walked Kelsey and Josh to their car.

"I'm going after her," Philip said.

Josh, looking dejected, nodded. "I know. I'm coming with you."

Kelsey started to protest, but Philip cut her off. "If I need backup, I'll call you."

She glared at him, but kept silent.

"They sold her. You heard them. She could be anywhere," Josh said. "Frank Evans knows. We have to go there. They might be holding her there."

Philip shook his head. "They wouldn't. I doubt Evans even knew they had her." He squinted, his eyes flashing rage. "But he knows now. His men would've alerted him. He'll know everything about her by now, including that I'm on my way to his place."

"So I want to go."

The vampire placed a hand gently on the young man's arm. "Thank you. But no."

"Then I'll go."

Philip and Josh turned astonished gazes on Kelsey. The shock on their faces reflected the shock on hers. She didn't know why she'd said that, but now that she had, it made sense. If she didn't, her son would likely sneak out again, and while she didn't want to do this because of something her son might do, she also wanted to help find Dakota. The girl obviously mattered to Josh more than Kelsey realized.

"You can't go alone. They're criminals." Another reason occurred to her then. "And Dakota might need a woman around when we find her." What if they'd already hurt the girl? Kelsey didn't want to think rape, but isn't that what these criminals did to young women?

To her surprise, Philip capitulated.

"We'll drop Josh at your place and head to Evans's." He stared her in the eye, but she didn't feel the tingle of hypnosis. "Just to be clear, I don't need backup. Dakota might need your help, so you'll wait in the car until I find her."

Considering how little she wanted to confront a crime boss in his own home, Kelsey readily agreed, but Josh protested.

"I'm going. She's my girlfriend."

The two adults exchanged glances and then gaped at him.

"Not officially," he whispered.

Kelsey cupped his face with her hands. "I know you like her, but I can't let you walk into a dangerous situation."

He met her gaze, solid and determined. "And I can't let you. We're wasting time. Dakota needs me." He freed himself from his mother's grasp and indicated the vampire with a wag of the chin. "She doesn't even know him. She only knows me—and you, a little. But she'll want me." His voice wavered on the last bit, but he drew himself up tall and thrust out his chest.

The motion reminded Kelsey how much taller than her he was. *Almost a man*, she thought for the umpteenth time that day. "He's coming," she heard herself say. "And we're both going inside with you."

When the vampire opened his mouth to speak, she interrupted him. "We're not your backup. We're Dakota's."

He shrugged. "I do the talking."

\*\*\*

Years had passed since Philip last visited Frank Evans at his home, and at that time, Evans lived in a much smaller house on a much smaller property. While the farmhouse the mafia head currently lived in looked like a simple brick bungalow on the edge of nowhere, an iron fence separated it from the road, and the gate across the driveway was shut and locked. Since Philip knew they'd lost the element of surprise after visiting the Owl, he pressed the button on the intercom. No one acknowledged them over the speakers, but the electronic gate slid open, and Kelsey drove through the entrance.

Silence hung over everyone in the car. Philip leaned forward in the front passenger seat, squinting to see as far ahead as possible. He'd removed his sunglasses and bandanna since the sun was down and no longer an issue. As the night deepened, his eyesight would sharpen, but here, the lane was lit with bright lights—and probably monitored with cameras. The driveway stretched a quarter of a mile from the road to the house. When they reached the building, Kelsey parked in front of the four-car garage next to a black Volvo.

"Big house," Kelsey commented.

No one responded. Wordlessly, they climbed from the car and walked to the front porch. Kelsey and Josh hung back, letting Philip ring the doorbell. The chimes had barely faded before the door swung open, and a woman in a maid's uniform, her brown hair pinned back into a bun, ushered them into the house.

"He's expecting you in the den." She spoke as if she assumed they knew where that was, but she led them to their destination anyway.

Philip took a good look around as they passed a circular stairway leading up to the second floor, walked by a formal living room on the left, a closed door on the right, then a powder room, kitchen, formal dining room, and finally reached the den. The maid opened a set of double doors onto a warm, cozy room finished in dark wood and glowing with firelight and tiffany lamps. The marble fireplace was trimmed with the same dark wood that paneled the walls, a bookcase loaded with books on either side of it. Bookcases covered the entire west wall, and in front of them stood a couch on which sat Nicholas Sabatino and two of Evans's goons. Evans sat near the fireplace on one of the three leather armchairs grouped around a low, teak coffee table. An oriental rug covered the hardwood floor.

Evans met Philip's gaze and raised his brows at the sight of Kelsey and Josh. "You brought company."

As soon as their boss spoke, the two goons stood as if preparing for action, each resting a hand on the gun tucked into his jacket. Beside Philip, Kelsey sucked in an audible breath and took a step backward as if she recognized the two men. Philip had seen them before, mostly with Sabatino. Both men wore black suits, were clean-shaven, and had short hair. The taller one had black hair, the other guy brown. Any semblance of respectability ended there. Each man sported a teardrop tattoo on his face and three dots at the base of the thumb of his right hand. *Mi vida loca.* Philip wasn't impressed.

"Relax, fellas. We're here to chat."

Both men glanced from Sabatino to Evans, as if uncertain what to do. The maid appeared then with a bar cart and offered them drinks. Philip kept his expression neutral and shook his head. "Nothing for us, thanks."

Kelsey and Josh remained silent, letting Philip speak for them. Was it trust in him or fear of the mobsters that had mother and son stepping back? Perhaps since the missing girl was Philip's daughter, they allowed him to be the alpha in this meeting. Josh's expression was grim, his lips pressed together as if he barely controlled a desire to speak. Philip took it as a show of respect that the boy refrained from confronting Evans—respect, or wisdom.

Evans accepted a scotch, as did Sabatino. The maid ignored the two thugs. Philip assumed she'd been instructed not to serve them alcohol, and there was nothing else on the cart except a bottle of blood.

"Suit yourself," Evans said. He inclined his head at the two henchmen. "Wait outside while I visit with my old friend and his … guests. Close the doors behind you."

After the men stepped into the hall and shut the doors, Evans motioned for the visitors to sit. Philip strode to the armchair across from Evans and sat down. Kelsey and Josh moved to the sofa, perching on it as far from Sabatino's side of it as possible.

Philip got right to it, but he kept his voice even and devoid of the rage simmering inside him. "Where's my daughter?"

# CHAPTER 17

Evans cleared his throat and, when he spoke, kept his gaze fixed on Philip. "First off, I want to say I had nothing to do with this." He glanced pointedly at Sabatino. "Nicholas unwittingly acquired your daughter in a business transaction and then re-homed her before he discovered her relationship to you."

Philip's grin at that declaration chilled Kelsey's heart. The vampire didn't move, didn't break eye contact with the one-eyed man, but it felt as if the room's temperature dropped twenty degrees.

When Philip remained silent, Evans continued. "He attempted to retrieve the girl as soon as he found out. You must believe he did everything he could, but they'd already delivered her to her forever home. I'm so sorry, my old friend." He paused there, letting *my old friend* hang in the air between them.

Just how old was the relationship? The man wore a lapel pin designating him as human with some psychic gifts. That and his missing eye verified he wasn't a vampire. A vampire's eye would've regenerated. The only outward sign of Philip's distress was an involuntary flexing of his right hand into a fist. He just as quickly uncurled it, letting the hand rest on his thigh. He still said nothing, so once again, Evans babbled into the silence.

"She's safe. She's fortunate, actually—"

It was Josh, not Philip, who broke into the man's soliloquy.

"Fortunate?" The young man jumped to his feet, his face red, his fists clenched. As he took a step toward Evans, Sabatino also leaped to his feet and moved toward Josh. This caused Kelsey to rise and stand between her son and Evans's second in command.

The vampire snarled in Sabatino's direction, while Evans motioned for Josh to sit.

"Young man—I'm sorry, I don't know your name."

Josh ignored the passive-aggressive request to identify himself, and Kelsey internally cheered her son's courage.

"She's my girlfriend." He frowned, but then continued. "I don't care how you say it; you bought her and then sold her into slavery. You had no right."

"Son."

"I'm not your son. We're not on familiar terms. You kidnapped a teenage girl. Perhaps the police would be interested to know you do this."

Kelsey placed a hand on Josh's arm. Threatening a mob boss with arrest wouldn't help them get Dakota back. Kelsey didn't know what he was capable of, and while she trusted they were safe as long as Philip was with them, when they left here, they'd be on their own. The less anger they raised in Frank Evans and his posse, the better. All she wanted now was to leave here and forget they'd ever met Dakota Lawson and her father. And Frank Evans and his men—though the two goons waiting outside in the hall would remind her of this visit every time they showed up to collect their protection money from her. She'd recognized them the moment she'd stepped into the room, and, of course, she'd recognized Sabatino from pictures on the internet. The man was semi-famous, mostly for nefarious reasons. She had no desire to stay on his radar.

Evans chuckled. "My relationship with the police keeps me in business. Son."

Josh scowled, drawing an amused smile from Evans. "Please, I have no intention of letting this degrade into a pissing contest. Stop the ego displays, boy. The young woman in question wanted to go to her new home."

"You're lying," Josh said, his tone low but firm. "She asked me to help her escape."

"That was before she understood the deal we offered her."

"What deal?" Finally, the vampire jumped back into the discussion. When Josh opened his mouth to protest again, Philip waved him into silence and told him to sit. "Don't make me ask you again, or you and your mother will have to wait outside."

Kelsey scowled at the vampire, but kept her mouth shut. She'd wait until they were away before verbally thrashing him for how he'd spoken to her child. To her surprise, Josh, looking apologetic, sat back down. Kelsey followed suit.

"What deal?" Philip repeated, returning his attention to Evans.

"Quite a sweet one, according to Sabatino. She's

betrothed to someone with high standing, and she sees the advantages. He'll be good to her. You'd be pleased with the match we made."

"Quit fucking around, Frank. No more euphemisms for what happened to my daughter. Your men bought her and sold her. Who'd they sell her to? She's out of your hands. You've got your money. As soon as they paid you, your part in this ended. So if I go after them, none of it's on you."

"It will be if I tell you who they are. I'm not about to destroy my reputation to recover one dhampir girl who's content to be where she is."

Philip rose, prompting Sabatino to also get up. Once more, Evans waved his second down. As the vampire approached, Evans flipped the patch up from his missing eye. "You want to mesmerize me? You want to break our pact, my friend? After all these years? After what—"

The vampire froze in mid-stride, but he kept his gaze leveled at Evans. "After what you did for me?" He averted his gaze, scanning the room. He walked to the bar cart and picked up the bottle of blood. "Real or synthetic?" he asked, without a hint of interest.

"Always real."

"We'll never return to what we were. My friend." Philip set the bottle back on the cart and turned to face the mobster once more. "I won't mesmerize you. I don't have to."

This time it was Evans who looked away, slipping the patch back over his eye socket as he did so. "You know I can't betray my client. But I do have something for you that might make you feel better about the girl." He tossed a quick glance at Josh, but when he spoke again, his attention was back on the vampire. "Nicholas has a video-recorded message from her. Explaining the situation. I viewed it, of course, to make certain she didn't reveal her new home."

Josh once again interrupted the discussion. "If she's so happy with all this, then why can't we know where she is?"

"My client's situation is unique. No one can know where or who he is. You'll have to take my word for it."

Josh glared at Philip. "Are you buying this? It's bullshit. He sold your daughter. Who knows what they're doing to her. You can't leave her with them."

Philip strolled to Sabatino and held out his hand. "The message."

The man rose and fished in his jacket pocket, retrieving a memory stick. He handed it to the vampire, who accepted it but stared into Sabatino's eyes as he did. The man's gaze softened and his jaw slackened.

Kelsey couldn't take her eyes off the scene, though she wanted to look over at Evans to gauge his reaction.

"Where is she?" Philip prodded gently.

"No longer in this world," Sabatino replied.

# CHAPTER 18

Everything went to hell the moment Philip entranced Sabatino. Evans raced to the vampire, calling out for his bodyguards as he did. One moment Kelsey stood watching the vampire hypnotize Sabatino, and the next, she was struggling with one of Evans's goons as Josh tried to fight off the other. She hadn't heard them enter the room, hadn't noticed their approach until one snatched her up from the sofa while the other grabbed Josh. Kelsey never saw what the mob boss did, but suddenly Philip lay on the ground, thrashing and crying out in pain.

"Let me go." Kelsey tried to kick Tall Guy in the shins, but he easily dodged it and punched her in the gut, dropping her to the floor.

"Mom!" Josh sank to his knees at her side, giving up his fight with Shorty.

Kelsey gasped for air as her son put an arm around her and made soothing noises. The concern on Josh's face touched her, and she leaned into him. While her breathing slowed, she took in her surroundings.

Tall Guy and Shorty stood over Kelsey and Josh. Neither had weapons out, but that was probably more a factor of how small a threat mother and son posed. Philip lay on the floor, unconscious. Kelsey's heart jumped, and she got to her knees and was about to rise to her feet when Tall Guy put a restraining hand on her shoulder.

"Stay."

She snarled at him. "I'm not a dog." She tried to rise again, but the pressure on her shoulder kept her down.

When Josh made a move to get up, Shorty pulled his gun.

"Stay," Tall Guy repeated. "I insist."

Evans, who loomed over Philip, poked the vampire but got no reaction.

"He dead boss?"

In the moment it took the mobster to reply, Kelsey's breath stopped and her pulse roared loudly in her ears. What would they do to her and Josh if Philip was dead?

Evans shook his head. "Out cold."

"What did you do to him?" Kelsey shouted.

"Injected him with colloidal silver."

"Why?"

"I didn't know how else to stop him without killing him."

She met Evans's gaze. "You didn't want to kill him?"

He shook his head. "We're friends. In a way."

She tried to process that but couldn't. "What way?"

"Long story."

A moan from Philip interrupted them. Evans motioned for Sabatino to take the two bodyguards and leave the room. The second in command hesitated, causing Shorty and Tall Guy to glance uncertainly at the doors.

"Boss, I—"

"It'll be fine. Leave. If you're not here, he can't use his voodoo on you. He wouldn't want to hurt these two"—he waved toward Kelsey and Josh—"and he won't hurt me."

"You sure?"

Philip stirred and his eyelids flickered.

"Go! Now!" The desperation in Evans's tone and his anxious expression compelled the men to move. They left without another word, shutting the doors behind them. Kelsey took the opportunity to get to her feet, and Josh also stood up.

The vampire opened his eyes.

\*\*\*

The fire in his veins had diminished enough to allow coherent thought to return and his muscles to relax so he no longer writhed on the carpet at Evans's feet. Philip gulped air into lungs that wouldn't process it, but it felt good to do it anyway.

"Give it some time." Evans continued to hover over Philip, who turned his head so he could see what Kelsey and the kid were up to.

The two huddled on the couch, and the fear in their eyes told Philip they wouldn't be any help. They couldn't do more than cling to each other. Had Kelsey even tried to see if he was all right, or had she focused on protecting Josh without a thought for Philip's condition? And why should he care? Her priority should be her son, as Philip's should be his daughter.

"Dakota." Her name slipped out as a croak between

chapped lips. A chug from that bottle of blood would flow like sweet nectar down his throat right now. He scanned the room until he spotted it on the bar cart. On the other side of the room. Might as well be a million miles away. His body weighed him down. He wouldn't be zipping anywhere anytime soon.

His tongue darted out in an attempt to moisten his lips. That damn dryness was killing him. Perhaps not literally, but if he didn't drink soon, the thirst would become hunger.

As if reading Philip's mind, Evans strode to the bar cart and picked up the bottle of blood. "I know you want this." His gaze met Philip's. "You ache. It won't go away, and when the thirst turns to hunger, you won't be able to stop yourself. You'll have to have it— or something like it." He looked pointedly at Kelsey and Josh.

"W-what …?" He couldn't speak, couldn't get up.

"He injected you with colloidal silver," Kelsey blurted out.

Evans gave her a dirty look but made no move toward her.

All Philip could manage in response was a croaking wheeze.

"I'm sorry," Evans said. "I had to do something, and the only way I know to disable a vampire is the silver injection. You gave me no choice." As he spoke, Evans gestured with his hands, waving the bottle around as he did.

Philip remained silent, but not by choice. His gaze followed the bottle's trail. His mouth grew drier, and his hunger deepened until it became painful lust. He opened his mouth, and fangs sprang from his gums.

"Oh, God," Kelsey cried out in despair, punctuating

it with a groan.

"It'll be fine," Josh said, but he glanced uneasily in Evans's direction. "You said he won't hurt me and my mom." There was pleading in the young man's voice.

"I said he wouldn't choose to."

"What does that mean?" Rage replaced timidity in Josh's tone.

"He'll have to feed. It'll be up to you whether I give him this bottle of blood or lock you in the room with him. Either way, I'll guarantee you won't interfere with my business ever again."

A hissing sound, as of air leaking from a bicycle tire, escaped between Philip's lips. He could smell the humans, especially Josh, who was young and ripe. A growl started low in the vampire's throat, and his eyes rolled back in his head. Evans bargained with Kelsey and Josh, but Philip heard only the hum of their voices, not what they said.

He hauled himself to his hands and knees. Soon, he'd be ready to stand. Soon, he'd be ready to leap— to Evans, of course, because he had to try for the bottled blood first, and he had enough sense to lunge at the bad guy. But if that wasn't enough …

The doors slammed and a lock snicked into place.

Philip shook the blur from his eyes. Evans had vanished. Kelsey stood, her body blocking Philip's view of Josh. In her hand she held the bottle of blood. Her eyes were terrified, and the hand holding the bottle shook. Despite all that, she crept closer and sank to her knees in front of him.

"You have to sip it. Let me help you."

# CHAPTER 19

Red. It filled the bottle Kelsey held in her hands, the bottle the vampire crouched before her reached for, but which she kept just out of his grasp. She refused to let him snatch it from her. She had to control his intake or he'd gulp it down and then attack her or Josh for more.

"Can you hear me?"

His response was a hiss and a growl, but his pupils cleared a little. He stared at her, but she refused to look him square in the eyes. If she did that, they'd be as lost as if she handed him the bottle and let him chug.

"I'll take the cap off. Josh, get me a glass."

When she heard no movement, she risked a glance at her son. He sat frozen on the couch, his gaze riveted on Philip.

"Joshua Roland Davis! Get me a glass. Now."

That snapped him out of it. He rose to his feet, his face as pale as a vampire's, sweat beading his brow. He moved with caution, as though he feared he'd stumble, but he moved quickly enough that she didn't need to shout at him again. He brought her a rocks glass and held it out for her.

"You hang onto it. I'll pour."

Philip's pain-soaked, raspy voice interrupted. "Hurry. Can't hold back."

As the blood trickled into the glass, Kelsey caught the scent of it, faintly metallic, and almost gagged.

"Mom, take it."

She snatched it from her son before he dropped it, and the moment it left his grasp, he raced to the wastebasket next to the desk at the back of the room and retched into it. No time to worry about him—it was only a bit of puke and served Evans right for abandoning them here.

"Drink." She held the glass out to Philip, who snatched it and gulped it down.

He passed the glass back to her, licking flecks of blood off his lips as he did. "More."

She steadied her hands and poured another round into the glass, which she noticed now was crystal. Somehow, that made it worse, and while the blood looked nothing like juice, she knew she'd never want to drink anything red again.

He slugged back the next ration and once more returned the glass to her. "Again."

Uneasy, she checked to see how much remained in the bottle. She figured she had enough to give him two more glassfuls. After that, he'd either control himself or attack. She checked Josh's current location. He sat on the floor by the wastebasket, his head in his hands. Good. Philip would go for the closest human, and she'd make sure he reached for her first. That might give Josh enough time to escape. How difficult would it be for him to break down the doors?

"Again." Philip wiped his mouth with his sleeve and held the glass out to her.

Before she filled it for the last time, she said, "How do you feel?"

"Pour." He drew his lips back in a snarl, revealing his fangs, which hadn't retracted.

"Pull in your fangs."

"I can't."

"You're gonna."

His knees gave out, and he slid sideways and then rolled to rest on his ass. The glass had slipped from his hand, but it didn't break since the distance to the ground wasn't far. The carpet provided further protection.

She snatched up the glass and held the bottle over it, ready to pour. "I'll pour if you show me you can retract your fangs. Come on. You can control yourself. You told me you can. You survive on animal blood and donations. Retract the fangs."

Was she pushing her luck? She knew little about vampires and whether they were quick to anger or helpless against their urge to feed. Philip had told her he hadn't fed on a human in years. Surely he'd had enough of the blood to have recovered control of his addiction—or whatever this was. *A basic need for survival.*

"Okay. Yes." His chest heaved as he sucked in air. He opened his mouth in a silent scream, and the fangs slid back to hide within his gums.

Some tension drained out of Kelsey then, and she almost swooned.

"I'm pouring the last of it." She did so and then held the glass out to him.

He took it from her, but not as frantically as he'd done with the other servings—another good sign. He drank, slowly this time, his Adam's apple bobbing as he swallowed.

The bottle slipped from Kelsey's grasp and rolled a short distance away across the carpet. She rose to her feet and backed away from the vampire, her gaze fixed on him, watching for any sign that he'd attack. She shuffled to Josh's side. "Get up and go to the doors. Try to get them open."

A voice from a speaker hidden somewhere in the room interrupted her. "Well done. Tell the vampire the deal, Ms. Davis, and you're free to go."

*Evans.*

She scanned the walls near the ceiling and spotted the camera. He'd watched them the entire time. She turned to verify Philip's location, when he reared up before her.

"What deal did you make on my behalf?" The whites of his eyes were tinged with pink, and his brows furrowed in anger. His lips parted, and with a snick, his fangs slid out again. "Tell me, darling, what the fuck you've agreed to."

# CHAPTER 20

Heart in her throat, Kelsey stepped backward and bumped into Josh.

"I …" She couldn't continue and guiltily averted her eyes from Philip's.

"What did you do?" he asked, his voice low and steady.

Evans piped up again. "Tell him, Ms. Davis. You're not leaving until we finalize this deal, and Philip needs to be aware of the terms."

"What did you do?" This time, he'd raised his voice, but it remained controlled.

"We agree to leave here and stop pursuing whoever has your daughter, and Evans will ensure our safety."

"He'll ensure *our* safety?" Philip responded.

"We want to go home," she whispered. Tears sprang to her eyes.

Josh put a hand on her shoulder. "What about Dakota, Mom?"

She turned her back on the vampire, though it made her nervous to do so, and gripped Josh's upper arms.

"She's her father's responsibility."

Behind her, Philip said, "I agree. Which is why you had no right to make any kind of deal on my behalf."

She spun around to face him, her face flushed and her hands fisted. "I had no choice." She spit out the words. "He had us. He still has us. What do you think we can do?" She shook her head. "I want to go home with my son and forget we ever met you or Frank Evans. I can't go up against a crime boss."

"You assume a great deal, Ms. Davis. I'm a businessman. An entrepreneur."

"Right. Which is why you have us captive in this room and why you bought and sold Dakota as if she's property." She dropped her fists, walked to the doors, and jiggled a handle. "Open it. We're leaving. Whatever this is, is between you and Philip. We've got nothing more to do with it."

"Oh, but you do. You gave me your word. I gave you the blood. So now you're responsible for whatever Philip does. If he continues to pursue this matter, I'll have to hold you responsible. As we agreed, if you recall."

As she had before, Kelsey made the promise, figuring she could handle Philip and his objections when they were safely away. "I promise, okay? Let us go."

"Kelsey …" Philip began.

"Not now. Will you quit arguing? We need to leave. Now. In one piece." She looked over her shoulder at him. His lips were pressed together, so she couldn't tell if his fangs were out. *Who cares? At least he's not trying to bite our necks.* "Let us out. We'll make a lot of racket busting out of here if you don't. Do you want your family to hear it?"

The response was a chuckle. "They've heard worse. Belanger, listen to your human."

Kelsey scowled at that, but remained silent. The vampire met her gaze and gave a single nod. "Open the doors."

"I take it you agree to the deal?"

"Just open the doors."

"You agree? I'm recording this, and I want your agreement on record."

"Or what? You don't let us leave? Who'll stop me?"

"You know what the deal is. You'll leave, and no one bothers you again."

"No one better bother me regardless."

Kelsey stepped over to Philip and grabbed him by the shirt. "Listen," she hissed under her breath. "Agree with him."

"You're always safe, my friend," Evans said. "It's the woman and the boy whose safety is in question. If you don't care about them … well, renege on the deal and see what happens."

Kelsey's eyes widened as the fear she'd felt all night ratcheted back up to terror level. "Philip." She didn't say anything else, but the pleading tone did the talking for her.

Philip cursed but finally relented. "Open the doors."

"Do you—?"

"Yes, I agree. Open the damn doors."

"A moment."

The room fell silent. Kelsey put a hand on Philip's arm and opened her mouth to say something reassuring, but he cut her off, his voice slightly above a whisper. "This isn't over."

\*\*\*

The doors swung open, and the trio stepped into the hallway, Philip taking the lead. He stopped in front of his old friend and glared at him. "Never ask me for anything again."

"I'm not the bad guy here. You'll understand that when you view your daughter's message."

"I doubt it. If she's speaking under duress, I'll know, and if she is, whatever deal we have—whatever deal we've ever had—will be void."

"You willing to risk these two on a hunch?" Evans waved at Kelsey and Josh and shook his head. "I don't think so. You'll see." He stared at Philip a moment, then said, "Get the facts, my friend. Or you'll always regret it."

Philip pushed past the syndicate boss, and without waiting for his companions, stalked to the front entrance and outside. Kelsey grabbed Josh's arm and pulled him along, racing to keep up with the vampire.

Relief had flooded through her when she realized Evans was indeed letting them leave, but anger now replaced the relief. The vampire blamed her for this? Seriously? After she'd saved his life—probably—giving him the blood in small doses so he wouldn't die or force-feed from her and Josh?

When he reached Kelsey's car, Philip stopped and whirled around to face them. "You had no right to speak for me," he said through gritted teeth.

At least the fangs weren't visible.

Kelsey scowled, stormed up to him, and unable to stop herself, shoved him. "I had every right to protect myself and my son. You had no right to drag us into this mess."

"If you recall, Josh dragged me into this." With an apologetic glance at Josh, he said, "I'm not saying I'd prefer he never told me. Dakota's my daughter." He thudded his fist on the car's roof, but not hard enough to dent it. "Damn it, you've hamstrung me. If I continue the search for her, they'll hurt you."

That deflated her, and she felt sorry for the man inside the vampire who'd lost his only child. When she replied, her expression lost its fury and her voice gentled. "What would you have had me do? If I'd refused the deal, he'd have locked us in there with you without leaving the bottle of blood." She placed a hand on his arm, and he allowed it. His face contorted in grief. "We had to get out of there. I think we can keep looking—"

"No." He shrugged off her hand, and the rage returned to his expression. "I gave my word."

"We'll work around it." She remembered the memory stick with Dakota's message. "Shouldn't we view the video first?" Hope laced her voice. "Maybe we'll see something in it that'll tell us where she is, who has her."

He sighed and touched her cheek with his hand. She shivered from its chill and he dropped it. "I'll take it home and let you know what I find."

"No!" Josh said. "I have to see it. She's my ... my girlfriend."

Philip's lips quirked, but if he found Josh's declaration humorous, he squelched the grin that threatened. "Very well. Take me to your place. Less likely to be bugged."

Kelsey stared at him a moment, wanting to ask him a dozen questions, but, in the end, she got in the car without a word.

# CHAPTER 21

When they arrived at Kelsey's apartment, she was tempted to send Josh up to his room and take the vampire into the store for a private talk, but she didn't want to relive what had happened earlier. Instead, she led the little party up the stairs into the apartment and told Josh to call his father. When her son protested, she insisted.

"You lied to him and took off on us twice in one day." She glanced at her phone. "He's left me more than one message, and I assume he's left at least as many on your voicemail. Call him, tell him you're fine and you're sorry—again—and then join us out here in the living room."

As soon as he made a move toward his room, she strode into the kitchen and took the bottle of white wine from the fridge. As she took a wine glass from the cupboard, she addressed the vampire. "I guess you don't drink wine."

"I can."

She shrugged, not interested in vampire physiology

enough at this point to ask him how that worked. She only said, "So … you want a glass?"

"No, thank you."

She slanted him a look. "Don't judge me."

His face registered surprise. "For what?"

"Nothing." Why get into it? She wouldn't know where to start, but everything about today made her feel guilty, as if everything was her fault, even though she knew it wasn't. *Because it isn't. I had no control over any of it.* And that's what she had to change right now.

So far, she'd reacted to what others had done. Josh, Philip, Evans, and Blair. They all had made things happen, and she'd reacted. Blair had the least responsibility for anything that had happened tonight, but he wasn't in the clear. Josh had lied to his father about staying home, and Blair hadn't verified with Kelsey. She'd learned Josh had gone rogue from a vampire.

She poured an extra-large helping of wine into her glass and set it on the counter. Should she offer the vampire something else? If he could drink wine, could he have anything else?

"I don't have any blood." Horrified that she'd unintentionally brought his attention to the fact that yes, she had blood, but it was coursing through her veins, she added, "Bottled blood. I don't have any. No reason to. I never expected to have a vampire up here."

"Slow down, darling." He clicked his teeth at her. "I don't bite."

"Well, do you want something else?" She opened the fridge again. "Milk? It's almond. Or there's water or juice."

He chuckled, a deep rumble. "I'm fine." He sobered then as he pulled the memory stick from his pocket.

"Let's get on with it."

She led him into the living room and powered up her computer. Josh rushed from his bedroom, cell phone in hand. The phone was off.

"Did you talk to your father?" Kelsey checked the time. Almost 1:00 a.m. "Was he still awake?"

"Yes, and yes."

"What did you tell him?"

"The truth. That I was searching for my girlfriend."

"What did he say?"

Josh dropped onto the couch and watched his mother log into the computer and plug in the memory stick. "He was mad I lied to him, but he understood I wanted to find Dakota." He rose and walked to the desk. "She's in danger."

"Yes, but you didn't have to lie to your father about it."

"I know. I said I was sorry. I'm sorry I lied to you both. I should have asked for Dad's help instead."

She let that drop. It was probably better that it played out the way it had. At least this way, she'd been there for Josh instead of obliviously going about her day while her ex and her son chased gangsters.

She double-clicked on the video file and opened it. The video showed Dakota, frozen in place, a large arrow centered on her chest to indicate where Kelsey needed to click to run the recording. The girl's brow was furrowed, her large blue eyes shiny with emotion. Her hair flowed loosely around her shoulders, the light in the film giving her skin and hair a golden cast. Kelsey's gaze was drawn to the young dhampir's lips, which were slightly parted and showed no evidence of fangs. If she hadn't had the lapel pin on her collar to declare her mixed breed, Kelsey would never guess the girl was part vampire.

Philip reached across Kelsey to drape his hand over the mouse and click play. The video reset to the start of the recording and panned out to show Dakota seated on a metal and plastic kitchen chair. Nothing in the background revealed where she might be. The room appeared empty, the wall behind her a neutral cream.

*At least she's not tied to the chair and she's dressed.* Kelsey glanced at Philip and then at Josh. Both scowled at the screen, their eyes riveted on the girl before them.

Dakota wore a long, emerald gown with gold trim. Like something out of a medieval fairy tale, Kelsey mused.

A male voice spoke off-camera, and Dakota's gaze shifted to somewhere to the right and off-screen. She gave a slight nod. "I understand. Do you?"

The same male voice replied, "Agreed."

She turned her attention back to the camera trained on her and spoke. "Father, they want me to explain to you that Mother didn't sell me. She received a dowry in exchange for my marriage to a prince whose name I'm not allowed to reveal. We're to wed in secret, as it would be too dangerous for the news to get out too soon. I can't explain further, but I want you to know I've agreed to this.

"Please tell Josh I'm sorry things can't work out between us. The nation needs me to do this, and I understand." She dipped her chin as though drawing on inner reserves. When she looked up again and stared into the camera, she thrust out her chin and her hands gripped either side of the chair's seat.

"No one has harmed me. No one will harm me. I'll be safe, and you'll hear of me in the future. The news will be good, and you'll be happy for me. I'm sorry we've never met, and I don't know if we ever will."

When she stopped talking, the male voice asked her if she was finished, and she vehemently shook her head. The camera zoomed in for a closeup.

"Tell Josh ..." Her voice broke then, constricting Kelsey's heart. "Tell Josh I'm sorry. I'll miss him forever, but it must be this way. He shouldn't search for me, because those who asked for this marriage will consider that a threat to their kingdom. By the time you hear from me again, Josh might be long dead of old age, so please, Father, give him my message. I heard you're searching for me too. Please stop, but understand it means the world to me that you cared enough to trouble yourself. Goodbye for now."

The recording stopped, and the image they'd seen when they'd first opened the file froze the girl in place once more. When Kelsey turned her gaze to Josh, she discovered tears trickling down his cheeks, and he sobbed silently. She turned to look at Philip. His expression was fixed in a murderous rage.

# CHAPTER 22

Silence filled the room. Philip closed the video and ripped the memory stick from the computer's USB port.

*Thanks for safely removing the hardware* popped into Kelsey's mind, and she cringed as soon as she thought it. Of course he wouldn't think of removing the memory stick using the safety protocol when his daughter had just bid him farewell for what sounded like, at the very least, Josh's lifetime. Kelsey waited for the vampire to say something—anything—but he remained quiet.

Josh wiped away his tears and stared dejectedly at the computer's desktop, which displayed a picture of Kelsey and Josh smiling into the camera. Kelsey quickly initiated the computer's shutdown process so the vampire wouldn't have to see their happy faces at what was probably one of the worst moments in his life.

"What should we do?" She didn't really want to continue the search. Dakota herself had told them not to, but what if whoever had taken her had coerced her to say what she'd said? They'd never know if what they'd heard on that video was the truth unless they hunted Dakota down and asked her. But that would mean putting themselves at risk for a girl who claimed she didn't want to be found.

"We? Oh, no, darling. There's no more 'we.' We're done."

He strode toward the exit, and the movement jarred Josh from his silence.

"Stop! You can't leave."

Philip paused. He turned, a sad smile on his face, and studied the boy. "You can't help me anymore," he said, his voice gentle and filled with compassion. "You can't help her."

Kelsey wondered if he purposely avoided saying Dakota's name.

Josh's lips trembled, and when he spoke, his voice wavered. "You can't abandon—"

"I'm not," the vampire cut in. "But you're dropping it."

"No." Kelsey rushed to his side and put a hand on his arm. He shook it off, his face a mask of rage. Rather than scare her, it made her more determined to talk him off whatever ledge he'd stepped out on. "If you're thinking about pursuing this, you could use help. We could help you."

"You heard her. If you or your son interfere, you'll endanger your lives. Didn't that sink in? Are you that thick?"

She ignored the insult. If this were her child, she'd lash out at Philip in the same way. They were virtual strangers entangled in an untenable situation. Whatever they did was likely the wrong thing. Drop the search and, if this was a lie, Dakota's life was destroyed. She'd likely suffer for decades, if not centuries. If they continued the search, they could, all three of them, lose their lives. And if Philip searched on his own, he'd risk all their lives, but Kelsey would have no control over any of it.

"They don't need to find out we're still hunting." She stared into his eyes, consequences be damned, but he turned his head, severing the budding connection.

"What do you mean?" The rage had disappeared from his voice, replaced by curiosity and hope.

"What if we search indirectly? Compile clues. Plan strategy. We could search in secret, and when we have a direction, we'll establish who we need to talk to. But we can at least figure out a direction first. We could start by examining the video for clues. No one need know we're doing it. Information gathering only."

The vampire contemplated her words, and after a moment, turned toward the door again as if about to leave. Kelsey pressed her lips together, refusing to argue with him, refusing to offer her help again if it wasn't wanted. But if whoever had Dakota didn't learn right away the search for her continued, he'd find out eventually, and their lives would immediately be at risk. If the vampire didn't appreciate what she did for him, he could stuff it.

He scrubbed his face with his hands and sighed. "Okay, darling, let's do it."

\*\*\*

On the northern tip of the state of Skanadario, Dakota Lawson settled into the captain's chair at the head of the eight-seat mahogany dining table. Directly across from her sat her betrothed. He looked regal and handsome, as he had every time Dakota had seen him. But this time, they were alone.

Gone were the men who'd brought her here. Wherever here was. It sent shivers down her spine to think of it, and she didn't know for sure, but they'd quite possibly brought her into faerie country. Today, she intended to find out. If she went along with this, they owed her full disclosure.

The table before her held a spread fit for a queen— or, in this case, queen-to-be. In front of her sat warming trays filled with eggs done in various ways, home fries with a side of gravy, pancakes, waffles, a cauldron with oatmeal, a plate stacked with toast— whole wheat and multigrain—and condiments to go with it all. A variety of fresh fruit rounded off the meal.

They hadn't forgotten drinks. Coffee, tea, juices, and water were all on offer on the sideboard next to the dining table. Also on the sideboard sat platters of sweet delicacies: assorted pastries, muffins, and cakes that made Dakota's mouth water just to see them. Their aroma made her stomach gurgle.

They also hadn't forgotten she was part vampire. A large carafe of blood stood by her plate, along with a tumbler to pour it into. If she wanted to skip everything else, she could drink her fill of blood. Dakota didn't know whose blood it was or from where it came, so she decided that was as good a place as any to start.

"Where'd you get the blood?" She leveled her gaze at him.

He smiled, and she tried to read whether he meant to mock her but failed. His green eyes mesmerized her, and she slipped into a dream world where the two of them held one another and danced to music only they could hear. When he spoke, his voice woke a yearning in her she couldn't identify; she only knew he alone held the key to satisfying it.

"It came from a human, my dear. Is that acceptable?" Concern laced his voice, and they turned and spun around a garden fragrant with lilacs and roses. Sunshine through the surrounding trees traced a golden path for them. She felt light on her feet, and she wondered if it was the lovely emerald slippers they'd given her to wear or if it was this strong, beautiful male who infused her with such grace as she'd never had.

"I don't want anyone hurt on my account."

He pressed his lips to hers, and she let him, though she'd never let any male kiss her that way before. It felt soft and tender and tasted of strawberries and sin. When he pulled away, she hungered for more.

"No one will suffer over you, dear heart. I'll make sure of it."

"Then where did the blood come from?"

He spun her around again and then dipped her. His lips hovered over hers, and she ached to feel them on her—anywhere on her, please, but he never even skimmed her chin. As he raised her to standing, a void hollowed her, and she pressed her body against his in an attempt to fill it.

"How'd we get here?" She rested her head on his shoulder—his strong, solid shoulder.

"We're here, and we're not here."

She understood. They still sat in the dining room at the palace.

"Will you tell me …?"

"Anything," he whispered.

That surprised her. She'd expected him to evade her

questions.

"Why me?"

He kissed her again, this time more urgently. She felt hunger in it, and it flared a response in her body. Blood coursed through her loins, making her ache. Her panties grew damp, and her breath hitched. Dizziness made her cling to him, had her fisting his shirt in her hands.

A moan escaped her, and he pulled away enough to hover his mouth over hers, so temptingly close but so out of reach.

"Please."

"Please what, my pet?"

She gulped. A tear slipped from each eye. "I can't."

"Can't what?"

Frustrated, she let the tears stream, angry that he'd reduced her to this. "I can't be what you want. I don't understand what's happening to me. Why me? Why am I here at all?" When he didn't reply immediately, she added, "I'm nobody."

That made him smile, though it was kindly. "Not at all. You're you."

"You could have …"

"Yes?"

She drew in a long breath, calming herself and stopping the tears. With a sniff, she firmed up in her mind she'd never be their victim, and as soon as she did, she woke from the dream. Once again, she sat across from him—Culain Shiels, her betrothed—but the ambiance in the room had shifted. Somehow it made her less sad.

"You could have asked first."

He tilted his head to the side and studied her. "Indeed?"

Not knowing what to say, she said nothing.

"May I tell you a story?"

"Will it answer my questions?"

"It will."

"Then yes," Dakota replied.

# CHAPTER 23

Culain spoke, his tone soothing. "Once, the fae ruled in a permanent spring in various pockets of the world."

*The fae.* Dakota's guess had been correct.

"We didn't mix with other humanoids and didn't want to, but sometimes, well, let's just say the tales about changelings have a grain of truth in them."

"You stole babies?"

"Stole. I suppose you'd see it that way." He frowned. "Will you eat something?"

She shook her head. "Maybe later."

His expression became neutral. "Suit yourself." He continued his story as he loaded his plate with mounds of food.

"The babies needed us. They were in trouble. Beautiful and healthy, but they'd been born to parents who didn't want them or who mistreated them."

"Ah, you consider what you did a noble gesture."

"I do, but it wasn't completely altruistic. We needed those babies. They were our salvation. You see, we were in just as much trouble as those infants." He paused to shove a forkful of veggie omelet in his mouth. He chewed, closing his eyes and inhaling deeply as he savored the taste. When he opened his eyes again, he said, "Please, try something. It's absolutely delicious."

"Maybe later." She wasn't ready to eat anything the faeries offered. She refused to slam shut any possibility of escape, but she was getting hungry enough to want to eat her own arm. She'd had a chocolate bar in her jacket pocket, but they'd taken all her clothes. The only thing they left her was her own body. Damn faeries. So that's how they manipulated people into accepting food from them: starve them until they caved, and then they'd be stuck in faerie land forever.

"Suit yourself," he said again, then continued, "We raised them with kindness. They became one of us. Married our kind and continued our line."

"That's why you needed them."

"Yes." He hung his head, but the motion didn't cause her to believe he was dejected or remorseful. "We have trouble conceiving. Over the centuries, we raised our vibrations so high we lost our ability to reproduce. We faded from the physical world."

"But you're back in it now. Doesn't that mean your vibration has lowered? The unmasquing lowered everyone's vibration." She wasn't sure what all that meant, but she knew for certain it meant all hypernaturals were revealed to humans.

"If that's the direction it'll take, we haven't seen evidence of it yet."

"So can't you, you know, go out there, mix and mingle, and find a person to marry without kidnapping anyone?"

He dabbed a biscuit in a puddle of gravy and munched on it. "It's not that simple. We tried that. But our realm remains hidden. Your kind, the vampire half, unmasqued completely. My kind remains, for lack of a better term, behind the veil."

"How did the men who kidnapped me know where to take me? How'd I get here?" The journey into faerie land was a black box to her. She'd been unconscious for the entire trip. She neither knew how she'd gotten in nor how to get out.

"One of our own led them here, of course."

"And led them out?" She smiled at the thought that perhaps the men who'd kidnapped her were now trapped with the fae as well.

He grinned his understanding. "We had to. Otherwise, no one would deal with us again." His eyes grew unfocused, and for a moment, she thought he'd gotten lost in thought, but he picked up his story where he'd left off. "The human babies we raised lived with us, but they always had a yearning to leave. Every last one of them. No matter how we loved them; no matter how they loved us. Deep inside, they needed to go where the air was heavier, the ground firmer, the flames hotter, the water thick enough to drown in. Their spirits needed it. If they didn't get it, they died, eventually."

"The fae are immortal? Like vampires?"

He nodded. "The one difference is we can be killed as any human can, whereas vampires must be killed in specific ways. For example, a regular bullet will kill us. The touch of iron or steel causes us pain. Even so, we'll live forever if no violence ends us."

"And disease?"

"We're unaffected by disease. So far, to my

130

knowledge, we don't get sick and never have."

"What happened to the humans who wanted to leave?"

"We had to let them go again, and to our kind, it was like losing loved ones to death. We couldn't live with them on the physical plane, and they could never return to our world. Once they leave here, they never come back."

"Then why hold me prisoner? You let humans leave when they wanted to, so why force me to stay here?"

"Because we can, and because, once you get to know me and understand our people, you'll be happy to stay."

*Cocky bastard.* She glared at him. "I have a boyfriend."

"No, you don't."

She glared at him again but didn't argue the point. Technically, she and Josh hadn't been a couple, but that was only because he hadn't had the chance to ask her before the faeries stole her. Dakota found herself reaching for a piece of bread and caught herself in time. "One thing I don't understand: How did you leave here to get babies if you can't return once you leave?"

He shook his head. "We can. The fae can. Humans can't. It's a one-time deal for them. And when they leave here, after years of living amongst us, eating our food"—he looked pointedly at the feast spread out before them—"they change, stop aging normally. Time here is different. So they leave to be with their own kind only to find they've changed too much to return to their human lives. Decades or even centuries have passed, and their families are long dead. When they try to come back, the way is shut forever. They get no second chance to live with the fae."

Dakota rose and started pacing so she wouldn't slip up and eat something. She moved as far away from the dessert table as possible. "I still don't understand what this has to do with me. I'm not even human."

"Exactly."

She went to one of the long, narrow windows in the room and peered outside. The gardens below grew lush with colorful plants and green foliage. Tall trees and sparkling fountains added shade and interest. Two tabby kittens bounded around a koi pond, trying to squeeze tiny paws under the netting stretched across it to protect the fish inside. As he talked, she kept her gaze on the scene outside.

"The unmasquing changed our lives again. You see, half-fae babies were also half human, and we lost many to the mortal world as soon as they grew to adulthood and felt its pull. But the unmasquing also brought us the dhampirs."

She thought she understood now. "You didn't want me for me. You wanted me for my race. What do half-vampires give you that humans can't?"

His chair scraped the hardwood floor as he pushed it back and rose. His footsteps trod lightly across the room, drawing closer and closer to her post at the window. The kittens below, failing to reach the fish in the pond, gave up and wrestled one another. Dakota giggled as they tumbled about.

Culain brushed her cheek with his finger. "You're so beautiful. I didn't pick you simply for your race. I picked you for your beauty, your high spirit, and your mind, Dakota Lawson."

"How would you know anything about me? I'm nothing. I'm nobody."

His hand slid under her hair and cupped the back

of her neck. He leaned in close to her, his breath light and tickling on her cheek. "Not nothing. Not nobody. You're a princess."

"I'm not."

"You're engaged to me, which makes you a princess the moment we marry. The formal title is yours to use right now." He kissed her cheek tenderly. "They showed me your picture. You were golden and beautiful, and you were healthy."

Dakota raised her eyebrows and tilted her chin down. "Healthy."

"Yes, healthy. A perfect, healthy, half-human-half-vampire girl. Dhampirs are closer to fae than they are to humans. Your vibration is higher than that of humans. You can enter our world, and if you leave, the way back isn't closed to you."

She could leave. The knowledge soothed her. They'd let others leave. "And the passage of time?"

"Normal, for you. You don't lose centuries."

"Even if I ate your food?" She knew that's why humans lost centuries in this world. They changed physically after eating the food here, after drinking the water and breathing the air.

"Even then."

She could leave here and see Josh again. Still, how could she know Culain told her the truth? It could be a trick.

"Why tell me all this?"

"Why keep it from you?"

She shifted to face him, her lips dangerously close once more to his as he angled his head down to meet her gaze. "To make me eat and trap me here."

He kissed her forehead, sending a jolt of electricity down her body straight to her loins. She stifled the moan that tried to escape. God, why did he have to be so beautiful? Why did he attract her so much it hurt her physically to be near him?

"I want you to stay. I want you to want to stay." He stroked her cheek, and her knees almost buckled.

She straightened, locking them, and steadied herself with a hand on the window frame. "They kidnapped me. It makes me want to escape." Why had she said that? Now he'd watch her all the time. Or he'd have her watched all the time, which would be even worse.

"I'm sorry they did that to you. I wanted you, Dakota, and I couldn't go out there to meet you. They had to bring you here. If I'd have sent you an invitation, would you have come?" He brushed her cheek again.

"I ..." No. She wouldn't have come. She'd have refused him. "Maybe if you asked nicely." There. That should satisfy him. It was a lie, but it was a white lie. Then something else occurred to her. "You saw a picture of me, and you had me kidnapped."

"I saw a picture of you, and I had you investigated. The information I received made me choose you."

Her stomach constricted as she remembered the mermaid girl she'd tried to rescue. "Were there others?"

"I had several candidates to choose from."

Dakota shoved him, throwing him backward a few steps. He made a startled sound in his throat and grabbed after her as she twisted away from him and ran to the door.

She pressed on the handle, ready to fling it open. It was locked. She sank to the ground in despair.

# CHAPTER 24

Culain crouched beside Dakota and put a hand on her shoulder. "Please, let me help you."

"Help me?" She twisted to meet his gaze, and the rage and despair warring in her eyes squeezed his heart.

He'd wanted her for so long, even as he argued with his family that this was wrong on so many levels. Somehow, he'd have to make her understand even though he himself did not.

"You said you'd tell me a story. That was a stupid story." She sounded like a child, and he reminded himself she hadn't lived long in this world though she'd aged as if she had.

"It's the story of my people."

"They made me send a video to my father. To my boyfriend."

The way she said "boyfriend" sent a surge of annoyance through him, but he brushed it aside. Because of him, his people had ripped her from her life. It hadn't occurred to him she might love another.

None of the intelligence gathering they'd done indicated she had a boyfriend.

"They made me tell them I wanted to stay and to stop searching for me."

"Did you mean it?"

"I had to talk as if I did. They threatened to hurt my father and Josh if I didn't do what they wanted." Sobs choked her again, and she buried her head in her hands.

Culain sank down next to her. They must look like quite a pair, both in their fancy attire sitting on the floor as if they were children playing with toys. He had a momentary flash of sitting before a fire, pushing a toy carriage with a dashing doll coachman while his brother trotted a toy highwayman on a toy horse toward Culain. Back then, they'd never heard of humans, and their mother still lived.

He sighed and put an arm around Dakota. She tried to shrug it off, but he eased her head onto his shoulder and stroked her cheek, gentling her as he would one of his horses. "Shh. It'll be all right. I promise."

"Sir?" A tap on the door followed the query. The lock snicked, the handle jiggled, and the door rattled as the serving man tried to open it.

"Come back later," Culain hollered, irritation overpowering his voice.

The door settled against their backs, and this time, the lock didn't turn to trap them in here.

"He's still outside. The door's not locked, so he's still outside," Culain said.

Dakota lifted her head, a puzzled expression on her tear-stained face. "Don't you have a key?"

"No."

"They locked us both in?"

"Afraid so." He shifted so they could look into one

another's eyes and see the truth or the deception in what each said. "I'm in this the same way you are."

"You're forced to marry me?"

He nodded. "It's easier for me, I admit, because I had a say in who they brought me." He rose and offered her his hand. She accepted, and he raised her so they stood face-to-face but at arm's length.

"Who's doing this to us?"

"My father. The faerie realm. It's complicated." She had no idea how complicated, and he had no time to explain it to her at the moment. Right now, he needed to convince her to drop any thought of escape. Though she was a stranger to him, he cared what happened to her, and death by a firing squad of archers wouldn't be her fate if he could help it.

"Why don't you rebel?"

"I'm a prince. My life isn't my own." How could he make her believe her life was now no longer her own? He'd been raised a faerie prince. He'd understood his destiny from the time he learned to speak. One day, he'd known, his family would find him a mate, and he'd marry her. Whether they loved each other was secondary to the female's perfect biology. Not many girls ticked all the boxes but Dakota did.

Perhaps he ought to tell her now. "According to the analysis, you're my perfect mate."

Her mouth dropped open, and he couldn't decide if the accompanying expression was horror or disbelief. Perhaps a mixture of the two.

"What analysis?"

"The DNA testing they did on you—"

"When? When exactly did they test my DNA?" The horror and disbelief had turned to rage, and he didn't blame her for getting angry, but she was making a reasonable discussion difficult.

He averted his eyes, ashamed of how much they'd done to her without her consent. He'd detested them for each violation, but for the greater good, he accepted it. She'd have to learn to do the same.

"Give me a chance to explain. Few women have your physiology. Your character. Your mind." He wanted to add "your beauty" but was reluctant to in case it made him appear shallow.

"Why me? Tell me, because you've dodged the answer to that question ever since we sat down to eat."

*You never ate.* But he kept that to himself as well. Sooner or later, she'd have to eat. He hoped to make it her decision. When she proved to herself he'd spoken the truth and it didn't trap her here, she might grow to trust him.

"You, because you're half human and half vampire."

"That much you've revealed. You wanted me for my race." She turned pleading eyes on him, and he wanted to scoop her into his arms and comfort her. But he refused to let himself feel so sorry for her that he'd help her escape. She had to stay. She had to marry him. Someday, she might forgive him for it and learn to love him, but that part wasn't important.

"You have certain traits that will give our children advantages. Your genetic makeup combined with mine will help them have exceptional health, intelligence, and leadership qualities." It excited him to think of it. He wanted to continue, to tell her that who she was would also make them exceptionally compatible as a couple, but the horrified expression had returned to her face, and she cut him off.

"Oh, God." She backed up, slamming into the

door. "I'm a broodmare to you."

"A crass way of putting it." He had an urge to slap her for saying it. He wasn't evil, and she made him feel as if he was. She was no saint. The fae doctors had verified she was a virgin, but she'd partied with her friends as much as any human teen. They'd brought her here just in time, prevented her from polluting her body further with alcohol, drugs, and the magick potions kids these days used to distract themselves. It made him feel like an old man even though he was only four years older in age than Dakota.

"You kidnapped me and plan to rape me. I call that crass—at the very least."

"I won't rape you." This time, he scowled in anger and hurt. How could she think he'd rape her? He'd never needed to force any female to sleep with him. Dakota Lawson wouldn't be the first.

"What if I refuse to have sex with you?"

"We can still have children, my dear. They'd be created in a test tube."

Her already pale face turned sheet white, and he had to grab her arm to steady her when she swayed. She pressed her palm to her lips and muttered, "I'm going to be sick."

She threw open the door and dashed into the hallway, but one of the two guards standing outside the room grabbed her from behind and pinned her to his body. She struggled in his arms, but he held her tight.

"Let me go. I'm going to be sick."

"Release her," Culain said. "I'll escort you to your quarters. We'll finish this later."

She went limp in the guard's arms, but Culain considered it a good sign that she hadn't, in fact, vomited.

# CHAPTER 25

Morning at the bookstore and café started off busy and helped Kelsey take her mind off the hunt for Dakota Lawson. Life almost felt normal again. Almost. The worry and fear over what Dakota might be experiencing while Kelsey went about her daily routine were never far away. A sick sensation had settled in her solar plexus and took up what Kelsey suspected was permanent residence. It gnawed at her, reminding her that every moment the dhampir girl was missing evidenced Kelsey's selfishness and narcissism.

"I'll take this one." Laura, the lycan, had returned. She placed the book she'd selected on the counter next to the cash register and smiled at Kelsey.

"Will that be all?" Kelsey said the words perfunctorily. She hoped Laura had found everything she'd wanted because Kelsey was in no mood to help anyone with anything. More evidence of selfishness?

"Yes, thank you."

As Kelsey rang in the purchase, she glanced dispassionately at the title—*Nurture Your Inner Wolf: The*

*Introverted Lycan's Guide to Assertiveness.* Unable to help herself, she smiled. "I didn't realize werewolves had issues with assertiveness."

Laura grinned back. "I know. We look all tough on the outside. I'm a pushover though. Especially at work."

Surprised she'd never considered what type of work a lycanthrope might do, Kelsey asked, "Where do you work?"

Laura hesitated. "I'm a vet."

"Like in the army?" It was the first thing that popped into Kelsey's head.

"No!" Laura laughed. "A veterinarian."

"You're an animal doctor?"

"Yes." Laura's smile grew broader. "I know it sounds weird, but I love animals."

"I guess it's not that weird," Kelsey replied.

Hurt flashed across Laura's face, and Kelsey regretted the implication behind her words.

"I mean, because you …" She had no idea how to finish that sentence without making things worse. "I didn't mean to offend you," she finished lamely.

Laura patted Kelsey's hand. "It's okay. I shouldn't have taken offense. I'm used to humans thinking of me as an animal."

"I only meant that your wolf side would provide you with great insights."

"I get it." She tapped her credit card on the machine Kelsey held out to her. "Don't worry about it. Your assumption was correct, so I can't get too offended." Laura hesitated, as if she had something else on her mind.

"Did you need something else?" Kelsey asked.

"Did you find the missing girl?"

Kelsey's eyes widened. How did Laura know about Dakota?

"The vampire who came in the other day and asked for your son. He was searching for the dhampir girl that hangs out here sometimes."

Oh, yes. Everyone in the store at the time had heard what Philip wanted. "He got a message from her. She's fine." At least, she hoped so. A white lie in this instance wouldn't hurt.

Kelsey bagged the book and dropped in the receipt. On a whim, she said, "Next time you come in, coffee will be on me. Maybe I could join you, and we could chat?"

"That sounds lovely." Laura took the bag and gave Kelsey another beaming smile. "See you later."

*She's so nice. Not like me at all.* It would do her good to make a friend from another species. To really learn about others.

"Have a great day," she said with enthusiasm, and she meant it.

*** 

Later that afternoon Kelsey welcomed Chase's arrival with relief. He joined her behind the counter and, oblivious to her angst, prattled on about his day.

"I'm worried about the exam I wrote yesterday, but today's potions exam was a breeze."

"Great." She grabbed her spray bottle of cleaner and a cloth, and bustled about wiping down the various surfaces before she went upstairs to wait for Josh to come home. Together they'd view a copy of Dakota's video and try to pick up clues from it.

"Yeah, I'm a natural at that. You want a potion, I

can mix it up for you. Kind of a basket-weaving course for me, but I tried to enjoy it while it lasted. I hear the next level is much tougher."

Kelsey froze in the midst of wiping a table. Magick. Could magick help them? Could they use it without detection? "Chase!"

He jerked his head in her direction, a startled look on his face. "Something wrong?"

Kelsey did a quick scan of the store. A few customers browsed the bookshelves, and two different groups clustered at the nearby tables. She gave the surface she worked on a final swipe and hurried behind the counter to his side.

"I need you to answer a question. Hypothetical situation." She kept her voice low, and when he replied, he matched her conspiratorial tone.

"Sure. What do you want to know?"

"Can you do a tracking spell?"

"Tracking spells are tough, but yeah, I can work a simple one."

"Would you do one for me? I'll pay you."

He hesitated. "Well, I'm not allowed to practice for money." His low tone dropped to a whisper. "I'm only supposed to do approved spells assigned for homework."

"Have you ever done one on your own? To learn on your own?" She hoped he had. It would make him more likely to break the rules for her. Guilt tweaked her conscience again, but it was for Dakota's sake. They had to find her quickly before something terrible happened to her—something worse than being snatched off the highway. Kelsey's mind easily filled in the blanks with numerous horrible scenarios.

He looked warily around the shop and leaned in

closer to her. "A few. To practice. Learn." He scanned the area again, verifying no one paid any attention to their conversation. "Unless you're some kind of phenom, you have to, but you can't always find an instructor to monitor it."

"Would you be willing to help me find someone?" Her turn again to search for eavesdroppers. Finding none, she continued. "It's important. A girl is missing." A girl Chase knew. "Dakota Lawson was kidnapped."

"Dakota," he whispered. "Of course I'll help you. Anything for Dakota. Anything for you."

Their gazes met, and she nodded. "Thank you. Can you come upstairs after your shift?"

"I have to go home first and pick up a few things, but then I'll come up. Does that work?"

"Yes." Suddenly, she felt lighter. They could locate Dakota, and no one would know they'd broken their promise to Evans. Not even Philip would know they'd found his daughter. She might not tell him. In fact, Josh wouldn't even have to know.

"Wait. Can we do this at your place? I could come by tonight." She bit her lip, trying to come up with a valid reason. The truth was valid enough. "I don't want Josh involved."

"Understood," Chase replied. "Come by my place after ten. We'll find Dakota, and then we'll go get her."

"Thank you," Kelsey said. And since Chase hadn't promised Evans anything, it would all work out fine. Right?

# CHAPTER 26

The video stopped and froze Dakota in close-up once more. Kelsey concluded they'd learned three major pieces of information from it: first, whoever bought Dakota had a long lifespan. Dhampirs were long lived. She'd said she was to marry someone high up. Her lifespan would factor into the equation.

Second, her pleas to Josh to discontinue the search for her, and her words at the start of the video, implied she'd made a bargain with her abductors. The girl obviously cared very much for Josh and wanted to ensure his safety, a fact which both touched and devastated Kelsey. Touched, because as a mother she instantly felt a connection to any woman who cared this much for her son, and devastated, because this woman had sacrificed her life to keep him safe. The layers of guilt continued to pile up.

Third, the dress Dakota wore and the words she used to describe her situation indicated a community that kept to traditional values and customs.

Josh, who sat next to Kelsey at her desk in the

corner of their living room, rose from his chair and paced the floor between the coffee table and the kitchen entrance. "I can't let her marry this guy— whoever he is. I guess he must have money." He stopped his pacing and, hands on hips, scowled at his mother. "She doesn't care about money. She wouldn't marry someone for his money."

Kelsey rose and went to him. "No one said anything like that. No one's thinking it. She's protecting you. Her father. She's a brave young woman."

"I don't want my woman sacrificing herself for me."

Kelsey resisted the urge to smile at how alpha male this made him sound. He'd get offended that she found this amusing when she wouldn't be smiling from amusement but from affection. "Honey, we'll do everything we can to find her, but you should prepare yourself for the possibility that she might speak the truth here. She might not want us to find her."

"Bullshit. Total BS. They made her say all that."

Kelsey waited a beat, brushed aside her son's cursing as a symptom of the circumstances—hell, she wanted to swear like a dock worker who'd been kicked in the balls—and took his hand. "We don't know why they took her, except they want her to marry someone. Someone who has position and power. It sounds like an arranged marriage." She didn't say that, based on what Annabelle and Marshall had said, it was more of a sales transaction than a betrothal.

"Her mother sold her."

*Yes.* "With an arranged marriage, the man's family pays a bride price for the woman. Not in all cultures, but perhaps whoever arranged the marriage lives in a culture for which this type of transaction is normal."

"It's not normal for us. For most of us. She's

dhampir. They don't do this."

"Her mother did, though, and she did it willingly."

"She did it for her own selfish gains, not because it'll benefit Dakota. She sold her daughter."

"I agree with you. The fact we must accept, though, is that Annabelle arranged a marriage for her daughter, and that's not illegal. Many cultures do it, and it's an accepted practice here."

"It wasn't always. Not here. Not before the unmasquing."

Kelsey walked into the kitchen and poured water into a glass from the cooler. She returned to the living room. Josh still stood where she'd left him.

She said, "Trafficking in humans was illegal before the unmasquing and it's illegal now. Dakota was never consulted beforehand in this instance, which makes it suspect, but arranged marriages are an accepted practice, and you can't—we can't—do anything about it if all parties agree to it, especially the two people getting married."

"It never mattered to me before. I never cared about what happened to others before." His expression was so woebegone she wanted to cry.

"That doesn't mean you're selfish or self-centered." She recalled how often she'd accused herself of the same thing lately.

"It means I'm thoughtless. Since it never affected me, I didn't think about it."

"Why would you?" She set the glass of water on the coffee table and took his hands in both of hers. "You care for this girl—I can see how much you care for her. On that video, I saw how much she cares for you." She paused, unsure how to continue, but she needed to speak before he interrupted so she barreled on. "That doesn't mean you'll end up together. Even if she were still here, you might not end up together. You're young yet. Both of you. You both still have so much growing to do, and her lifespan is much longer than yours. That alone would've made things difficult."

"What are you saying? That I should forget about her because we could split up someday? I should leave her to be married off? Raped? Because the moment whoever has her marries her, that's what'll happen. You think they won't have a wedding night? That what happens won't be against her will?"

"No. I'm thinking all the things you are." She picked up the glass she'd brought out. "Have some water."

"Water? You brought that for me?" He shook his head. "You have strange priorities."

"I want to do something to make you feel better. A drink of water will help calm you."

He took it from her, chugged it, and set the empty glass on the coffee table. "Wow, I feel so much better."

She sighed and turned her back on him. "I'm only trying to help."

"By telling me to forget the woman I love."

"No." She spun back around. "To face reality. We might have to let her go."

"Philip won't."

"Philip promised Frank Evans he would. We'll all have to drop it sooner or later. Even if we find out where she is and who has her, we might have to let her live her life with him." If she could convince Josh, and later, Philip, of this, then she'd be the only one sticking her neck out. She wouldn't even be in any danger, because with Chase's help, she'd do everything remotely, in secret.

What mattered now was to call off Josh and the

vampire, and neither one of them was the type to give up. While she didn't know Philip very well, she suspected he was stubborn—she'd seen evidence of it when they were at Evans's—but he also had good reasons for continuing the pursuit. This was his daughter at risk. It revealed a lot about his character that he refused to leave her to a fate that might be worse than death even though he'd never met the girl.

"I have to go out," she said. "For now, why don't you do some research on what we know? Do an image search on a still from that video and see if you can find a match on that dress Dakota's wearing. Maybe we can figure out where it came from or who typically prefers that style."

He perked up at that, and relief washed over his face. "Great idea. It'll narrow down the community where they might be holding her. From that, we can make a list of possible high-level leaders who are looking for a wife." He hurried back to the computer, already focusing on the task before him.

"Perfect. Text me if you find something. I'll try to get back before you go to bed so we can discuss it." She took her black leather jacket from the closet and put that on over her black T-shirt and black leggings. She slipped on a pair of army-style boots to complete the look. Before she walked out, she hesitated, suddenly worried that if he actually found a match on the dress that identified a species, he'd race out into the night on a mission of vengeance. "You going to be all right here, Josh?"

Already tapping his way through the video to find a good location from which to snag a screenshot, he glanced over his shoulder. "Sure. Don't worry. We'll figure this out and get her back." He squinted, studying her attire. "Who are you trying to fit in with?"

"What do you mean?"

He shrugged. "You look like you're in college."

"I'll take that as a compliment. Stay here, okay? No matter what you find? You'll text me if you get something, right?"

"Yeah, no problem." But his voice was distracted, his gaze focused on the computer screen.

"I mean it, Josh. You stay home and contact me if you get anything worthwhile. Got it?"

"Yeah." He waved a hand in her direction. "You can go. Chill. It's all good."

She stepped outside, locking the door behind her. She'd just have to trust he'd follow her orders. Perhaps by then, she'd have news of her own to give him.

# CHAPTER 27

"We'll have to be careful," Chase said. "Once we create the circle of protection, you must stay inside it." Kelsey stood with Chase in the bedroom within the apartment unit he rented with two other students. He'd bribed them to leave for the night, and they'd accommodated him, though one would return by midnight. She hoped she and Chase would be long done by then, but a roommate showing up prematurely was the least of her worries. Kelsey had never worked a spell before—had no knowledge of magick at all—and had always thought it the work of the devil.

She clasped the cross around her neck for a moment to draw comfort from it, but all it did was raise more guilt over what felt like a betrayal of her religion. Spellwork was blasphemy, but if it meant saving her son, then she'd just have to blaspheme.

In the center of the room, Chase had set up some tools on a round table to serve as an altar. Three candles, all white, stood in a three-candle holder at the top of the table. On the altar's left side, Chase had placed a small dish of salt, and right below it was a small bowl of water. On the table's right side sat an incense burner with a long incense stick poking out of it, below which was a tea-light candle in a plain glass holder.

At the altar's base rested a book Chase referred to as his BOS, or *Book of Shadows*, and a knife he called an *athame*. He picked up a sword he'd propped against the altar and said, "You ready? Once I cast the circle, you can't leave for any reason."

"At all?"

"You can leave if you know how to cut a door, but I'd rather not break the circle for any reason since you're a newbie."

"Okay. Go ahead and cast."

As he started walking toward the northeast corner of the room, she said, "Wait."

He peered over his shoulder, brows raised.

"Protection from what?" Her face reflected the worry in her voice. He'd told her repeatedly she shouldn't leave the protective circle. Would he summon demons to help them? No wonder her religion forbade spell casting.

"From unwanted energies." He inhaled as though breathing through irritation, and when his frown changed to a more neutral expression, he continued. "Sorry. I'm not used to explaining it to someone who's against it. It makes me feel as if my existence needs justification."

"It doesn't. I understand you're a natural mage."

"I don't consort with demons. I work with daemons."

"I don't understand."

He shrugged. "I know. You'll have to trust me. If you want to learn magick theory, I'll explain later. Right now, do what I say, or I'll stop immediately."

"We're here to help Dakota. Whatever it takes, I'll do it."

"You say so, but you must understand what that means. Leave judgment and negativity at the door."

"Yes. I'm sorry. I just want to find Dakota."

"So do I, but I won't rush through this or half-ass it for you. I won't let you suck energy from me with your negativity."

Had she displayed negativity? She'd asked for his help and willingly assisted him in setting up the altar. "I didn't say anything."

He squinted at her. "You didn't have to."

She nodded, accepting his judgment though he demanded none from her. "I'll work on that. I trust you." Even she heard the sincerity in her voice this time, and he visibly relaxed.

"I'm sorry. I'm nervous too. It makes me sensitive, and I shouldn't take it out on you. I know you have no experience with this."

With a catch in her throat, she replied, "Thank you."

He moved to the northeast corner of the room and held the sword aloft, one hand fisted on the hilt, the other on the blade, which he pinched between his finger and thumb. He closed his eyes, muttered something she didn't catch, and walked the room with the blade pointed up as though he used it to draw an imaginary circle. She surmised this would be the boundary she couldn't breach.

Chase went through several processes he never explained to her, but which she assumed, based on his words and actions, either solidified the circle he'd drawn, purified the space, or cast out bad energy. He also paused at each principal compass point in the space and called on elemental energies to join them in casting the spell. This made her uncomfortable, but she kept still and silent. As far as she knew, the four elemental spirits he called—air, fire, water, and earth— had nothing to do with demons. Perhaps the Catholic Church would frown on asking for their help, but they would frown on all of this, so she'd earned their disapproval the moment she'd asked Chase to help her. She silently promised to pray for forgiveness in church next Sunday.

*Maybe go to confession.* The thought made her uneasy. Would the priest forgive her or excommunicate her if she admitted to this? *Worry about that later.*

Chase returned to the altar. He crouched low enough to reach under the table and retrieve a basket he'd placed beneath it. From it he removed a scroll that, when he unrolled it, revealed a map of the territories on their continent. He reverse-rolled it until it lay flat on the table, and then placed four gemstones—white, yellow, brown, and gold—on each corner to hold it in place.

"The stones are all aragonite. They'll clear the ley lines and remove any geopathic stress from the map. Spells work on the principle of correspondence. I'm using objects to represent the actual areas we want to search."

She thought she understood what he meant, though the way he spoke implied he didn't realize how minimal her knowledge was in this area. She'd heard of using crystals in energy healing, but she'd never believed in that mumbo-jumbo despite the verifiable existence of mumbo-jumbo creatures. Why did she so stubbornly refuse to accept the magickals? She'd never examined her beliefs this closely before, much as Josh had never considered the reality of human—and other species—trafficking until Dakota disappeared.

"What if she's no longer on this continent?" Kelsey said, her tone as solemn and respectful as she could make it. Was she even allowed to speak? Chase hadn't said she couldn't, but she didn't know the rules of the spell-casting game.

When he didn't reprimand her but answered the question, she relaxed.

"I've got a scroll for each one. Right now, I need to narrow down at least the general area. Then I'll get specific." He retrieved a crystal dangling from a chain. The crystal was cloudy white, about four inches long, and tapered to a point.

"This is a pendulum." He held it above the map. Once again, he muttered something under his breath. Kelsey caught the words yes and no, and the pendulum swayed beneath his fingertips. He continued to mutter, but when he said the words "Dakota Lawson," he said them clearly and forcefully. Apparently, it wasn't important for her to hear what he said for the spell to work, but he didn't care if she caught the odd utterance.

As he worked, the air under the pendulum thickened and intensified above the map. It spread from the center and lapped out in soft waves from beneath the dangling crystal, which now swayed more and more strongly. Suddenly, it rose to horizontal and strained in Chase's hand. He allowed it to guide him, and when he stopped and checked the location on the map to which it pointed, he frowned and raised his eyes to meet her gaze. "We have a problem."

# CHAPTER 28

Activity in the bar section of Blood Shots typically reached its peak around eleven at night. Philip sat at the desk in the office he shared with his partner, listening to the sounds of revelry, and contemplated pouring himself a drink. Scotch, not blood. He felt a need for the bracing jolt and thirst quenching a mouthful of the alcohol would provide. Blood satisfied hunger, not thirst, so he never even considered reaching for the bottle of O-negative on the sideboard.

The door opened and Dwayne walked in, a giggling young woman bouncing in beside him. Philip was in no mood for Dwayne and one of his chippies tonight. This one had springy curls of red hair, looked barely legal to be in the bar, and was obviously drunk. When she tilted her head to gaze up at Dwayne with adoration in her eyes, Philip noted the bite marks on her neck.

*What a dick.* How many of these girls—and, legal age or not, compared to Dwayne and Philip, they were girls—had his partner gone through in the last month?

He never turned them, which would've been an enormous responsibility, though most of them wanted it. He fed off them, partied with them, led them on, and then dumped them for the next flavor of the week—or day. Naturally, he'd hypnotize them so they wouldn't see it that way. They'd leave thinking they'd dumped him.

Under his desk, Philip's hands curled into fists. "What do you want?" He couldn't keep the anger out of his voice and didn't care if Dwayne heard it. His partner, however, seemed oblivious.

"Wanted to show my new *chica* command central." He leaned down and ran his tongue over her lips, eliciting a throaty moan.

"She's seen it. Now beat it." Philip pushed back in his chair and rose. He'd get that drink after all.

Dwayne parked the girl on the couch and strolled to the bar. The two vampires reached it at the same time.

"You okay, buddy?" Dwayne asked. "You seem uptight."

Philip snarled under his breath. "My daughter's still missing. Of course I'm uptight."

"Lemme buy you a drink." Dwayne removed two glasses from the rack above the bar and grabbed the bottle of scotch. He poured them each three fingers and dropped an ice cube into his. Into Philip's he dripped from a pipette bottled spring water he retrieved from the bar fridge. He handed Philip his drink, and they moved away from the bar—Philip returning to the desk and Dwayne to the couch, where the girl had passed out.

"You fed on her," Philip said.

"Well, yeah. That's why I see her," Dwayne replied.

Philip couldn't keep the scowl off his face, and Dwayne couldn't ignore it. "Judging me? You?"

Philip gritted his teeth, keeping his fangs in by an effort of will. The mild irritation he always felt these days after spending time in Dwayne's company had become full-blown anger. Their relationship hadn't always been strictly business, but over the years, Philip felt more and more often that he'd outgrown his friend. *Just like Evans.*

Before Philip could respond to Dwayne's dig about judgment, the phone on the desk rang. He snatched it up, grateful for the distraction.

"Philip Belanger."

"It's Josh." The boy whispered, as if trying not to be overheard.

Instantly, Philip sat up straight. "Did you find her? Wait a minute." He cupped his hand over the mouthpiece and said to Dwayne, "Gimme some privacy. Take that girl to one of the back rooms if you aren't taking her home tonight. And she'd better have signed the release form."

Dwayne shook his head. "What the hell happened to you?" But he lifted the girl into his arms and carried her from the room, kicking the door shut behind him. Testiness had made Philip add that last bit. Dwayne always got the release form signed before beginning the night's revelries.

Philip returned his attention to the phone call. "Okay. Tell me."

"I'm not sure. I found something that might lead to her."

"Is your mother there?" Why wasn't Kelsey making the call?

"No." Again, this was said in a whisper.

"Why are you whispering?"

When Josh replied, it was in a normal voice, but it contained a tinge of excitement. "I don't know. I guess I'm feeling paranoid. Because they told us not to search. You don't think they'd bug our house, do you?"

Philip smiled. The kid probably felt like some kind of hero spy, perhaps imagining himself riding in to rescue Dakota from the bad guys. "They wouldn't have had time or opportunity for that. What did you find?"

"The dress Dakota wore in the video matches a style typically worn by the fae."

Philip took a sip from his drink and considered the implications of Josh's words. The fae kept to themselves, and even after the unmasquing, they lived in a realm outside of the physical plane. If they'd taken Dakota, rescuing her would be difficult. Time for Josh and Kelsey to step away. As a vampire, he could tackle these otherworldly creatures, but it would be way too dangerous for the humans.

"Where's your mother?"

"She went out."

Philip had raised his glass of scotch to take another sip but froze it halfway to his lips at Josh's words. He glanced at the time: eleven thirty. The glass finished its journey to his mouth, and he took a large gulp. This conversation required it.

"Where'd she go?"

"She didn't say."

Philip frowned. This sounded worse and worse. "You let her leave without telling you where she was going?"

"She's my mother. She kinda does whatever she wants."

"Does she make a habit of leaving at night without

saying where she's going?"

Silence. Then Josh reluctantly said, "No."

Philip cursed. What could Kelsey be up to? Probably something she didn't want at least Josh to know. It also likely had to do with Dakota.

"Can you track her phone?"

Delight filled Josh's voice. "I'd love to."

Philip had to chuckle at that. "Payback's a bitch, right, kid?"

"Right."

"Call me when you locate her."

"Will do."

Before Josh could disconnect, Philip said, "You do nothing else. Understood?"

"Yeah."

"Not 'yeah.' You don't call her, and you don't leave your home. Got it?"

"I got it." He sounded annoyed now, but too bad. The last thing Philip needed was to have to hunt down Josh as well as Kelsey before going after Dakota.

*Humans. You can't live with 'em, and you can't turn 'em all into vampires.*

He fired up his computer and, after logging in, opened a browser. Time to learn about the faeries and find out why they'd want a dhampir girl for one of their own.

# CHAPTER 29

"What's wrong?" Kelsey asked.

Chase set the pendulum down on the map and stood up straight. "She's not on this plane."

"What does that mean?" Fear dripped from each word. What had they gotten themselves into? A moment of resentment toward Dakota almost had Kelsey telling Chase to take down the damn circle and let her leave, but shame immediately followed. The girl hadn't asked for this, and if her friends or her father didn't care what happened to her, no one would. No one, not even non-humans, deserved what she'd gone through—was probably going through now.

The problem was Kelsey didn't know for sure that Dakota wanted to be saved. However, the only way to verify that was to ask her, and they had to find her first.

"She's with the faeries."

"Oh." She didn't know what else to say. She knew almost nothing about the faeries. They lived north of the city in their own world and kept to themselves.

Some of them crossed the barrier on occasion, as if they were sowing wild oats before returning to their own world forever, but Kelsey had never met one.

"It'll be tough to get to her," Chase said.

"Do you know how?" If he could get her into their world, she could find Dakota, talk to her, and return before Philip and Josh even knew she'd been gone.

"Yes, but it's not a good idea. Not for a human."

"Why?"

"It's risky. Humans go in there, they can get trapped forever, or for so long that by the time they return, everyone they've ever known is dead."

"Is there a way to go there and make sure you come back to your own time?" she asked.

While Chase had innate magickal powers, his DNA remained human, making him a hypernatural human. This meant he'd have the same limitations she would going into fae country. She couldn't allow him to risk entering there if she wouldn't allow her son to do it, despite the loophole in her promise to Evans the option offered.

"Yes, but not many can carry it off. Throughout history, you hear of humans disappearing through a faerie ring or portal. If they return to their side, it's instantly, and almost no time at all passes. I've heard of only one recorded case of that happening. Most of the time, they're just gone. Sometimes, you hear of a case where the person returns, expecting no time to have passed, but discovers they've lost decades or centuries."

"You know of documented cases like that?"

"I study this, so yes, I've read documented cases. The government studies these people. Before the unmasquing, they locked them up for the rest of their lives. Didn't want word getting out that this type of thing happened. Wanted to prevent panic in the general public."

"They do that now with UFOs. Maybe those are real too."

He raised his brows. "The government doesn't kidnap alien abductees, as far as I know. You believe in that type of thing?"

"No. Maybe. I'm only pointing out the similarities in the rumors around these things. Some people believe that the creatures everyone in the past thought were faeries were actually aliens."

"They were wrong." He changed the subject with a dismissive wave of his hand. "Whatever. Faeries exist. We know they do. We know where they live, and we know something about their culture. Those who study the fae for a living have photographed and documented research on the faeries."

"I'm not arguing with you. I know they exist. I didn't get much history on them in school, since when I was in school they were the least known new species, but they were a species everyone accepted existed. No one other than the government has proof of extraterrestrials."

Silence blanketed the room, and Kelsey peeked at her cell phone to check the time. Almost midnight. Chase's roommate would return soon. "We need to take down the circle, if you're sure you know where to find Dakota."

"I do, but as I said before, you can't enter the fae realm."

"I don't have a choice. I'm not letting Josh go."

"Dakota has a father. Tell him where she is and he'll go."

She hung her head, envisioning telling Josh and Philip Dakota's location. It would be fine as long as Josh agreed to stay here while the vampire went after the girl, but Kelsey was convinced Josh would demand to go along. He'd have to stay behind, that's all. As his mother, she'd order him to remain at home. If necessary, she'd—what? Confine him to his room?

*Look how well that worked the last time.* She couldn't control him. Short of tying him to a chair while Philip was gone, the decision would be Josh's. Unless she didn't tell him what she'd learned. If she told only the vampire, by the time Josh heard the news, Philip would be back, with or without Dakota, and Josh would have to live with the result.

With more confidence than she'd had all night, she said, "Tell me where she is. I'll inform Philip."

***

Philip appeared on Kelsey's doorstep, and Josh let him inside the apartment.

"Where is she?"

"Mom?"

"Of course your mom." Philip shook off the irritation. He needed Josh to hurry. What if that fool woman was already on her way to the faerie realm? He calmed himself with the reminder that she had no way of knowing Dakota's location. Josh hadn't talked to her, so Kelsey didn't know they suspected the fae had Dakota.

But Josh's next words showed him how mistaken that assumption was. "She's at Chase's. The guy who works for her? He's a mage. Well, mage in training, but he's a natural."

164

Philip cursed. "*Tabarnak*."

"What?"

"She's getting the mage to locate Dakota." Why hadn't he thought of that himself? Because he didn't associate with mages.

Philip opened the door. Time to broaden his social circle.

***

With the coordinates and the map in her possession, Kelsey said goodbye to Chase and returned to her car well before his roommate returned. The moment she sat behind the wheel, she called Philip on her cell phone.

He picked up on the first ring. "Kelsey? Where are you?"

"I have some news about Dakota."

"Where are you?"

The anger in his voice annoyed her, so she snapped back, "Don't you mean 'thank you'? Do you want to know where she is or not?"

"Right now, I want to know where you are."

"What difference does it make?" So why didn't she just answer him? Probably because he was being such a jerk about it. "I'm leaving Chase's right now. He's—"

"I know who he is. Where are you going?"

"Home. Do you want to know about Dakota or not?"

"The fae have her."

Kelsey's extremities went numb. If Philip knew that, then so did Josh. Now it was her turn to panic. "Does Josh know this? Where are you? Where's Josh?"

"Relax. He's with me."

That wasn't an incentive to relax. "Where are you?" She flinched when it came out a shriek and then jumped at a tap on her window. She looked up to find Josh and the vampire staring at her.

"Oh, for …" She shoved open the door and stepped out onto the street.

Philip immediately grabbed her arm. "What do you think you're doing?"

"Searching for your kid. What do you think you're doing?"

"Keeping you from doing something stupid."

She fisted her hands on her hips and glared at him. "What would that be?"

"You went off on your own and didn't tell me or Josh where you were going or what you were doing. Did you think I wouldn't figure it out?"

She leaned back, and the smile she gave him was mocking. "No, to be honest."

When he tossed her a dirty look, she eased up. After all, Philip knew where his daughter was. Kelsey could take Josh home and leave the rest to the vampire.

"I have a map." She held it out to him. "I wrote down the coordinates."

This time, he did thank her. "I appreciate what you did. We didn't have an exact location—just the knowledge she was with the faeries."

"What now?" She turned to Josh.

He wore a stern expression, his lips pressed firmly together, his arms crossed over his chest. He was obviously settling in for an argument.

"I'll go find Dakota. You and Josh go home," Philip said.

"Oh, no, you don't," Josh shouted. "I'm going too."

Kelsey sighed. "You can't this time. It's not safe for humans." At Philip's look of surprise, she said, "Chase told me. Humans can easily get trapped in there. I won't let you go, Josh. This is something we'll have to trust Philip to do."

"I know the rules. I can get in and out no problem." He thrust out his chin, projecting an air of defiance.

"Maybe I don't want you to come." Philip grasped Josh's shoulders, and before Kelsey realized what the vampire was doing, Josh's eyes went vacant and his jaw slackened.

"No!" She tried to break the trance, but Philip shoved her aside.

"Stay out of it. Do you want him to stay home or not?"

Josh would hate her if she gave permission to do this. When he found out she'd let Philip manipulate his memory, he'd be furious with her. But what choice did she have? Let him run amok in the faerie world, perhaps never to return? Besides, maybe he'd never find out.

"Okay," she said. "Do it."

# CHAPTER 30

Culain walked Dakota to her room, and after ushering her through the door, he bowed and left. The lock slid into place with an audible click, and while she didn't know for certain that Culain rather than a guard locked it, she held the fae prince accountable anyway.

When his footsteps faded away down the hall, she kicked off her shoes and curled up on one of the two padded armchairs next to the cheerful wood fire blazing in the enormous stone fireplace. If she weren't miserable and scared, she'd consider this a lovely, comfortable room. They'd outfitted it as if they knew her intimately, which creeped her out even though Culain had already revealed they'd researched her.

The bed was a four-poster. She'd always wanted one of those, and her mother had refused to spring for it. Many of Dakota's school friends had them, some with gauzy curtains such as this bed had. The rest of the room maintained that aura of princessy romance, boasting plenty of ruffles in her favorite shades of blues and pinks with white accents.

Candles, along with the fire, gave the room a soft, warm glow. Though the walls were stone, tapestries hung from them, and one entire wall was nothing but bookcases. She even had her own desk, wet bar, and en suite bathroom. While the decor gave the place a medieval feel, these faeries weren't off the grid.

The chandelier in the dining room ran on electricity, and she'd spotted the servants carrying cell phones, though she'd never seen them use the devices. Perhaps electronics didn't work here. As far as she knew, neither did the internet. She envisioned faeries sneaking off to internet cafés or libraries in Tkaronto to complete school assignments.

Did they attend school outside their own community? She couldn't recall meeting any fae in her classes. Perhaps they remained outside the physical realm in multiple ways. After all, they'd given her these bookcases full of physical books rather than a tablet with electronic books. Most of the books they'd left her were from genres or authors she most enjoyed, which meant her mother had aided in at least part of the research.

Her mother. The woman who'd given birth to her. The woman who'd betrayed her. Annabelle hadn't even discussed betrothal with Dakota. She'd sold her daughter and allowed the men who'd organized the transaction to kidnap and terrify her. Why couldn't they have involved her in the process? How different would things be if they'd introduced her to Culain and let her decide for herself?

*Mom didn't want to risk me saying no.* How much money had the faeries paid? It must've been a great deal, but because her mother hadn't let Dakota in on this, her father and Josh were now mixed up in it, and their lives were at risk. The practical thing to do would be to go along with this the way everyone expected. It would keep her father and Josh safe. Her mother would elevate herself from poverty, though Dakota considered that an incentive to escape. Part of her wanted to punish Annabelle and bring the wrath of the fae down on her for her daughter reneging on the contract.

So negative consequences for her mother wouldn't factor into her decision to leave. Josh's safety and her father's safety would. What about her safety? Culain swore he wouldn't hurt her. He insisted he wouldn't rape her, not even on their wedding night. Dakota shuddered at the memory of his touch, and it wasn't from fear or revulsion. If she stayed, she'd give herself to him eventually. Whatever spell they'd put on her made her want him so badly she ached. That knowledge gave her the final push she needed.

Her nerves settled with the decision made, Dakota's thoughts turned to strategy. The trick with the hairpins wouldn't work. They'd removed them and tied her hair up with ribbons and string rather than pins. A nuisance, but she was determined to find a way out. She'd just have to get creative.

Her stomach growled, reminding her she hadn't had anything to eat or drink since she'd arrived here. Soon, thirst would have her knuckling under, but Culain had told her the faerie food and drink wouldn't trap her here. Did it even matter? She was stuck here. No way would she find a way out before she had to eat or drink something. Shouldn't she get it over with?

She licked her lips, her mouth and lips feeling dry, her throat parched. It had taken all her willpower to refuse even a mouthful of food or a sip of water in the dining room, and now the memory of that tasty spread obsessed her. If they came and took her back to the dining room, she'd eat and drink all of it.

Dakota rose from her chair and tiptoed to the wet bar. Small, simple, and elegant, it stood tucked into an alcove along one wall. The cupboards were the same dark wood as the posts on her bed, and a glass-fronted bar fridge let her peek in to see the various bottles and snacks available. A faucet that resembled wrought iron, but wasn't, had a handle that allowed her to change the temperature of the water with a simple turn. She pushed the handle all the way to the right and flipped it up to turn it on. Water streamed out. Where was the source? Within the faerie realm? Or did they have to pump it in from a lake outside the faerie lands? If that was the case, then she wouldn't technically be drinking fae water. Right?

*Oh, what the hell. I have to drink something.*

She took a glass from the cupboard above the sink and filled it with water from the tap. Before she sipped, she switched on the bar's light and held the glass up to it. The water looked clear and clean. She put it to her lips, but hesitated to drink, even though her mouth craved it, and she fought an urge to chug the whole thing down. Carefully, she touched her lips to the water and flicked her tongue out.

Before she could stop herself, she sipped from the glass, and then she sipped some more. The sips grew faster, bigger, until she was gulping water. When the glass emptied, she refilled it and took it to her chair by the fire. She set the glass on the end table between the two chairs and pulled her feet up to hug her knees to her chest. Did she feel any different? She still wanted to leave and find her father and Josh. Her head felt clear, and her stomach continued to rumble and beg for food. Either Culain had told her the truth—at least about the water—or she wouldn't notice the effects until she returned to the real world and discovered centuries had passed and everyone was dead.

She experienced a moment of dread and terror at that possibility, but it only firmed her resolve. She'd rather live among … Who, exactly? Her father's descendants? She'd never met her father. As a vampire, he could still be alive even if centuries had passed, so that gave her something to hope for. Or her mother's descendants? Would they welcome her into the fold or seize the opportunity to give her back to the fae? Josh would be long dead. What would she do then? Look up his great-great-great-grandson and tell him she once had a thing for his long-dead ancestor?

*No. If they're all dead, I'll know Culain lied to me and leaving was the right thing to do.* But what if leaving proved he hadn't lied to her? Would they punish Culain for her escape? Would her disappearance devastate him?

*He chose me from what might as well have been a catalog of women. He doesn't deserve my loyalty.* Then why did she feel so damn guilty?

Best focus on the most important thing right now: escape. What did she know about the palace and the room where they kept her? Her first challenge was getting out of the room, but she was confident she could manage that. She only needed to find something wiry and sturdy, and she'd pick the lock. Her second challenge was getting out of the palace undetected, a much more difficult feat. She'd seen guards at entrances and exits in addition to the servants who seemed to be everywhere, and who'd turn her in the moment they saw her alone. She'd deduced that much from the way they treated her. Despite the expectation she'd be their future queen, they treated her more like a prisoner than the prince's fiancée. They trusted her about as much as she trusted them.

Dakota rose from her chair and scanned the room, from the dresser across from her bed to the desk—no computer—and accompanying chair next to the sitting area. She'd examined the en suite bathroom when she'd used it in the morning. It contained a vanity and enough lotions and potions to keep her sweet smelling and relaxed in the bath. It also had a cosmetics collection rivaling that of any movie star. Perhaps one of the tools would suffice as a lock pick.

She'd start her search in the en suite's vanity. Her mind made up, her conscience quiet, Dakota strode purposefully into the bathroom.

# CHAPTER 31

Sunlight shone in through the crack in the curtains and woke Josh. Momentarily disoriented, he couldn't recall why he was in his bedroom at his mother's place. He should've spent this weekend at his dad's place. Then he remembered the party he'd wanted to attend. It must've been a wild one because he couldn't remember much of it. Anthony could fill him in later—that is, if his friend was in better shape than Josh. He grinned, figuring they'd have a hell of a time when they compared notes after work. Today was Josh's first full day at his summer job, and he looked forward to starting.

Josh stretched and rolled out of bed just as the alarm on his cell phone alerted him it was time to get up. He wasn't hurting too badly if he was up before the alarm went off, even if only by seconds. He headed to the bathroom to prepare for the day.

\*\*\*

The aroma of frying sausages filled the kitchen, and Kelsey monitored them while she set the table for Josh. She'd already had a cup of coffee and half a piece of toast with peanut butter. The guilty never ate well, and it was all she could do to choke something down.

"Wow, what gives? We're having eggs on a weekday?" Josh strolled into the room and grabbed a piece of toast off the stack in the middle of the table. He crunched down on it, melted butter dripping onto his fingers.

*Damn.* She should've known he'd find this weird. Why hadn't she thought of a cover story? It took a moment, but when she finally replied, she didn't think he noticed the long pause. "We didn't get our Sunday brunch together." That part was true enough. "I thought we could do it this morning, so I got up early."

Was that too much? Did she sound like the liar she was? She only wanted to protect Josh. He'd have run off to the faerie world and, no matter what he promised, odds were good she'd never see him again. Who could fault her for taking preventative measures?

"Thanks. That's so awesome. I'm starving."

"You all ready for your first full day of work? Have everything you need?"

His face went blank. "I ..."

"What?" *Double damn.* Hadn't he organized his briefcase when they arrived home?

Before she could say anything more, relief flooded his face. "I did. We came home, and I got everything together." He contemplated a moment and then asked, "Where were we last night? Did we go out somewhere?"

For this, she had an answer prepared. "I picked you up from a party. Even though you should never have been out with friends on a Sunday night." She waited, hoping he'd settle into the false memory. The vampire had told her discussing events as though they'd happened would reinforce it. "You didn't even know anyone. They were all Dakota's friends."

"Oh, yeah. Right. Guess I can't discuss it with Anthony after all." He chewed a few bites of egg in contemplative silence, then continued. "Dakota wasn't there."

"No. She's with her father, remember?"

"Uh, yeah. Her father." He sounded dubious, making her heart pound with fear. "She only recently met him for the first time. I guess she wanted to spend time with him."

Kelsey nodded, too relieved to speak.

Josh again tucked into his plate of eggs and sausages, but when he noticed she wasn't eating, he paused and gave her a quizzical stare. "Aren't you eating anything?"

"I had something while I made yours. I didn't want to wake you until everything was ready, but I have to get to the store."

"Oh, sure."

She hoped this doubt and confusion he wrestled with would disappear. The vampire had given no warning about the hypnosis disorienting the kid. It made sense, but she didn't like it.

"Mom?" Josh asked, his voice soft.

"What's up?" She tried to sound normal, nonchalant.

"I want to ask Dakota to be my girlfriend."

Kelsey sucked in a breath and hoped he mistook it for shock over her son wanting a girlfriend. She'd play along. She had to, but this charade was making her feel sick. Not in all his life had she done something so duplicitous, so manipulative, to her son. It was all that vampire's fault. Him and his daughter. Both of them were nothing but trouble.

"What do you think she'll say?"

"I know she likes me too. She'll say 'yes.' "

"She's half vampire, you know." She let a note of disapproval tinge her voice. Just a hint of it, so he'd think she didn't approve of the match.

"I know. I don't care."

Kelsey patted his hand. "Well, if you don't, then I don't. Let me know how it goes." She picked up a piece of toast and nibbled on it, each bite like sand. She knew exactly how it would go: Josh would try to call Dakota and the girl wouldn't answer. When he called her at her father's, which is where the vampire had told Josh Dakota was now living, her son would learn the dhampir girl had left town to visit relatives for the summer. At the end of the summer, if Philip hadn't brought her home, Kelsey would tell Josh Dakota was engaged to another dhampir. She'd blame the vampire and tell Josh the marriage was arranged and Dakota had agreed to it. She didn't know what else to do. For his safety, he could never know what had happened to the girl.

God, how she hated herself for what she'd done to him. For what she'd let the vampire do. If their plan worked, she'd never have to see Philip Belanger again, and she thanked God in advance for granting her that favor.

*** 

When Philip wanted to, he could move as stealthily as

a wraith, and right now, he wanted to. Since it was broad daylight, he wore all the sun protection gear he usually wore, and it felt stifling, but better that than singeing his skin. The path he followed would take him directly to the faerie world. He need only step through the mushroom circle at the end of it—so long as he could find it. The damn thing moved around. He had a fair idea of how to detect it, but this was the first time in all his long years of life he had to bother with the fae. If it weren't for that wretched Annabelle, he wouldn't have to do so now.

She'd fleeced him that day she'd walked into his bar, but she hadn't swindled him out of money. What she'd stolen from him had been far more personal, and it had been a long con. He hadn't realized at the time she'd only wanted him for his seed. She'd walked into the bar looking so soft and innocent. He scoffed at how he'd fallen for the sweet-young-thing act. Dwayne had wanted to toss her out, but when Philip heard the raised voices, saw her frustrated and close to tears, he'd intervened on her behalf. She'd shown the proper ID and signed the waiver, and she'd been oh so grateful to Philip for letting her stay.

He hadn't intended for anything to happen between them—it'd been a long time since he'd had sex with a human. He'd learned a long time ago that most of them were nothing but trouble, but Annabelle had convinced him she was different. She never fawned all over him as many women who came to the club did. She spent an enjoyable evening in his company that night, but they didn't sleep together right away. No, they built up a relationship first.

Philip tried to push all that from his mind. He never visited those days in memory, at least not intentionally.

As soon as Annabelle got pregnant, she dumped him. Told him she wanted to raise the child on her own. She'd taken the child support he sent, which he'd have continued to send until Dakota reached the age of majority, but she refused to let him see his own daughter. Like an idiot, he'd gone along with it. He'd even been grateful that she'd taken on all the responsibility for her so-called accident. Now, he knew she'd planned it that way all along for the money she got for selling the girl. That explained why she'd wanted him uninvolved. If he'd built a relationship with his daughter, he might have discovered what she was planning and prevented the sale.

Rage simmered in him, and when Annabelle's face drifted into his thoughts, he wadded up a ball of spit in his mouth and horked it onto the grass. It landed bulls-eye in the ring of mushrooms. He'd reached his destination. Philip stepped into the center of the ring and vanished from the physical plane.

# CHAPTER 32

Escaping from her room wasn't as easy as Dakota had expected. In fact, it took much longer than she'd anticipated. By the time she found something with which to pick the lock—a ballpoint pen she dismantled—her time ran out. Just as she kneeled before the door to start working on it, footsteps approached, and she raced back to the desk. She stuck the pieces of the pen back into the drawer where she'd found it and slammed it shut as someone tapped on the door. She whirled around to face her visitor.

Culain entered the room, his expression showing surprise to see her sitting at the desk. Since he didn't comment on it, she kept silent as well, but it took all her effort not to stammer out excuses for why she sat there.

*None of his business. You don't owe him any explanation. The desk is here. I was snooping in it. That's all.*

To distract him from wondering what she might be up to, she scowled at him and let her voice betray anger. "I never said you could come in."

"Nevertheless, here I am. I gave you a warning knock."

"Is that how it'll be? You do what you want, and I have no say?"

"It's time for lunch. You're to join me in the dining room."

"To watch you eat?"

A frown flashed across his face, and his hands formed fists, but with a vast sigh and obvious effort, he calmed his temper. "Dakota, you need to eat. Please. This hunger strike isn't helping anyone, least of all you."

Did she detect more concern than anger in his voice? She rose, but didn't approach him. "I'm not hungry."

He strode into the room, and she flinched when, for a second, she thought he intended to strike her.

He froze at her reaction. "You think I'd hit you?" The disappointment and hurt on his face and in his voice made her flush hot with shame, and she averted her gaze.

"How would I know? We barely know each other. You could be a misogynistic psycho who'd beat his fiancée to force submission."

"That's specific."

Surprised to hear the grin in his voice, she jerked her chin up to find out what was so funny. His smile broadened when their eyes met.

"You find me amusing?" she asked.

He shook his head. "Not at all. I find you refreshing."

Stumped, she simply blinked at him.

"Fae women tend to be more reserved."

"You mean pliant."

"I suppose. They're raised that way."

She stepped toward him before she realized she wanted to be near him, and halted the second it dawned on her.

"It's okay. Walk with me. We'll talk over lunch."

"I'm not hungry," she insisted, but she lacked conviction.

He shifted closer to her, and when she didn't back away, he offered her his arm. Slowly, against her better judgment, she took his arm and walked with him out the door.

\*\*\*

Stepping into the faerie realm through the mushroom ring zapped some kind of electrical current through Philip but didn't hurt him or even slow him down. What did slow him down was the squad of guards that met him on the other side. They showed no surprise, as though they'd expected him, which made him uneasy. He considered taking them on but decided to wait. They might get him to his daughter faster than if he randomly searched for her.

"Fellas," he said. "A welcoming committee. How nice." He grinned at them, but they wouldn't see it through the bandanna. His voice turned mocking. "Take me to your leader."

Apparently, they mistook his meaning, because one of them stepped forward and said, "I'm the leader."

Philip chuckled. "Sure. I mean your leader. The guy at the top. The big kahuna." He received more pleasure than he'd expected from throwing slang terms at them he knew they wouldn't understand. "Well, lads? Which way to the palace? I want to visit my daughter. I hear she's going to marry some prince here."

The faeries shifted uncomfortably, their chain mail clanking as they did. They'd drawn swords, and just to be a sport, Philip kept the gun he'd brought tucked into his belt. He wasn't sure a bullet would kill a faerie, and he preferred to retrieve Dakota peacefully, but if need be, he'd wipe out every single one of them. Perhaps he'd try to turn one of them to see what a vampire faerie would be like. Probably it wouldn't work. He'd never heard of a vampire faerie before, but perhaps no one had ever attempted it. He sniffed the air, trying to scent their blood, but could only pick up a floral aroma. Or was that what their blood smelled like? So much to learn about this mysterious race and so little interest in doing so. His mind had wandered, and Philip didn't care to follow it anymore.

He strolled along beside the leader as if part of the team, but the looks they got from passersby told him he fooled no one. Purely to annoy, Philip asked, "You been working here long?"

The leader cringed and ignored the question.

"Got a name?"

The guy spared him a stony glance.

"We're not going to be friends? Dude. I come in peace. No need for rudeness."

When he still received no reply, Philip fell silent and checked out his surroundings.

They walked along a long path through a heavily wooded area. The trees were typical of what he'd find in the physical realm outside the faerie ring: elms, maples, birches, cedars, and pines. Short shadows casting toward the east indicated an afternoon sun, highlighting the time difference between this realm and the physical plane. The air here was light and breezy, and with the trees offering shade, Philip slipped his bandanna down.

The march continued for another fifteen minutes before the trail ended at a bridge across a seven-meter-wide river. On the other side, the path continued, but only for a short stretch. It ended in a latticed wood portcullis set into the stone fortifications around the palace. Who did they expect to lay siege to the place? Did they think an army would step through the mushroom ring? Perhaps they fought amongst themselves.

His so-called guards escorted him across the bridge, and when they reached the halfway point, the portcullis lifted. The one who'd designated himself the leader walked Philip through the entrance, across a courtyard, and through a heavy wooden door into a tunnel. If they intended to imprison him next, this would be where they'd have to part company.

"Where are we headed, darling?" Philip paused his steps. "I sense it's not to see my daughter." He kept his tone pleasant. No need to upset anyone, and no need to get excited himself. Until they displayed overt animosity, he'd keep their interactions friendly.

"Keep walking." The lead guard's tone wasn't as amiable as Philip's had been.

"I'm loathe to be difficult, but it's imperative I speak to my daughter. I want only a quick visit. You don't even have to provide tea and cookies."

The leader nodded to the two lackeys on either side of Philip, and they grabbed him by the upper arms as though preparing to frog-march him to their destination. They failed.

# CHAPTER 33

The day started out quite fair and pleasant for Annabelle Lawson. She and Marshall talked to a real estate agent in the morning, explaining to her exactly what they wanted in a house. All her life, Annabelle had wanted her own place. As a child, she'd moved around a lot, not just to another location in the same town, but to the city. Her mother needed to stay ahead of her crazy, abusive husband, and Annabelle supported her in that endeavor.

The last straw for Mom had happened when Dad beat the snot out of Annabelle for wearing pants to go outside and play. Girls, he'd raged at her, his face scarlet, should dress like girls. Then *smack*, an open palm across her face and she went sprawling across the kitchen linoleum. Her tears and her pleas and her apologies hadn't satisfied him, and he continued to beat her until she passed out. Her mother had cringed in the corner. She'd known better than to interfere. Doing so would make it worse for both of them, so Annabelle was grateful to her mother for keeping silent and still.

But that night, the two slipped from the house on silent feet with only one backpack of possessions between them and as much money as Mom could steal from Dad's wallet. It wasn't much—certainly not enough to support them for more than three or four days tops, but it was enough to get them bus tickets out of town and into a hotel in downtown Tkaronto. Her mother explained it would be more difficult for Dad to find them in the big city, and as long as they paid cash, they could hide out there for a while until they earned enough money to start over somewhere else.

Shortly after they settled in Tkaronto, Annabelle's mother met one of Evans's crew, and earning money meant working for the syndicate. Mom became an escort, and when Annabelle turned sixteen, her mother introduced her to the life. Her mother had died of a drug overdose six years ago, leaving the then twenty-year-old Annabelle to fend for herself. She'd continued the escort life, but determined to work her way out of it, either by taking up with a guy who could support her in a decent lifestyle or finding a way to make the money herself.

When she heard through the grapevine that dhampir kids were in high demand in the slave trade, she decided that avenue was her ticket to freedom. Dhampirs grew quickly through childhood, hitting the lucrative teen years within five years of birth. When she learned that Philip Belanger's bloodline carried extra value, she determined to snare him in her web and bear his child. The real fortune came when she discovered the faeries were searching for a dhampir girl to wed to their prince.

Her plot had worked perfectly until Dakota got wind of the plans and tried to escape before the deal went down. The issues grew far worse when she involved that boy and Philip. But once the money changed hands and Dakota was safely ensconced with the faeries, Annabelle relaxed, certain she'd seen the last of all of them: the boy, the vampire, and the dhampir. That the dhampir was Annabelle's flesh and blood troubled her not at all. After all, the girl wasn't human, and it wasn't as if Dakota was turning tricks—not that turning tricks was anything to be ashamed of. Annabelle had supported them on the income just as her mother had done.

On this gorgeous day, when Annabelle and Marshall returned from the real estate agent's office, they anticipated spending the afternoon sitting in the backyard celebrating the next phase of their lives. They entered the townhouse and headed for the kitchen, Marshall to get a beer, Annabelle to pour herself a glass of wine.

They found their way blocked by the vampire who'd hooked Annabelle up with Philip that fateful night at Blood Shots with a ruse of refusing her entry. Like any gentleman and business owner, Philip had stepped in and saved the day. As far as Annabelle was concerned, that ended Dwayne's involvement with the scheme, and she'd paid him handsomely for it.

"What are you doing in my house?" She tried not to show her fright, but Marshall let out a loud gasp, and even Annabelle could almost smell the fear dripping off him.

"I think you know," Dwayne replied.

"You got your cut." She stalked toward the kitchen, but as she passed him, he grabbed her arm in a tight, painful grip, causing her to cry out.

"You lied to me."

She twisted her head around to stare at him, open-mouthed. "How so?"

"You never told me who the buyer was."

She shrugged. "Who cares? You got paid." She'd gotten the better of Evans's boys too. They hadn't known Philip was the father when they received the request for Dakota from the faeries, but she'd been the one to tip the faeries to the girl's existence. For a nice, fat finder's fee. If she hadn't been too terrified to leave Evans's crew out of the deal, she'd have dealt directly with the fae. Unfortunately, she was in too deep with the mobsters, and they took their cut as middlemen in the transaction.

"You've put me at risk. I think that deserves a larger share."

Annabelle snarled her rage at him, her mouth twisting, her eyes blazing. "We had a deal. I paid you fair and square."

"Yes, but that was before Evans learned the girl belonged to Belanger."

"That wasn't a problem when you helped me manipulate him into my bed."

"Because you were supposed to keep it to yourself."

"And not collect child support? I needed the money." She saw an opportunity as his fingers eased up on her arm, and she wrenched from his grasp and stormed into the kitchen. He'd completely ruined her good mood, but she still intended to have that drink. She opened the fridge and took out a bottle of white wine.

Footsteps followed her into the room, but it was only one pair that did. She whirled around to face

Dwayne. Marshall still stood in the foyer, afraid to enter his own home. What a wimp he'd turned out to be. In a way, she missed the three months she'd spent with Philip. He was an excellent lover. A wealthy man. He also had his scruples: he'd never have agreed to sell Dakota no matter how much money she drew. Annabelle was lucky he hadn't torn her and Marshall to shreds when he found out what they'd done.

"What do you expect from me? Evans will never learn of your involvement."

"And Philip? I deleted Dakota's message from his voicemail and impersonated him to lure her to the bar. Things could've gone very wrong if I hadn't intervened. If Philip finds out what I did, we're all screwed."

"Why would he find out? You planning to tell him?" She sneered at him.

"Careful. I'll tolerate only so much from you." He drew closer to her. "I want another ten thousand."

"No. You're out of it. We had a deal, and I paid you. I suggest you leave. You wouldn't want Philip to find out you were here. Where is he?"

Through gritted teeth, Dwayne replied, "That's my problem. The idiot's out hunting for Dakota. How long before he puts together that I had a hand in all this? He already questioned me about it. This'll blow up in my face, and I'll have to do worse than I've already done to him."

"Feeling guilty? Honestly, it surprises me when you vampires get all sentimental."

"We've been friends a long time." He said it defensively.

"And yet you betrayed him."

He snarled. "I had to."

She shrugged. "We all do what we have to." She retrieved a wine glass from the cupboard and poured a generous helping of chardonnay. Before she answered Dwayne, she gulped from the glass. "You're not getting any more money out of me—not for this kid. Tell you what," she said. "How about I cut you in on the next kid? Care to be a daddy?"

Behind them, Marshall at last came to life. He rushed into the room and grabbed Annabelle with two fists, scrunching up the blouse she'd carefully ironed that morning. "No more vampires." He shoved her against the fridge, her wine sloshing over the rim of the glass she held. He whirled on Dwayne. "Get out. Stay out. We're done. She's done with all you animals."

Dwayne growled, his lips pulling into a snarl that revealed pearl-white fangs, but he turned his venom onto Annabelle. "Sleep with you? You disgust me."

Her breath hitched and her chin trembled. "How could you?" But the hurt then turned to anger, and she screeched, "How dare you?" She set her glass of wine, half of which now speckled the floor, on the counter and folded her arms across her chest. "You want money or don't you?"

Marshall latched onto her arm with a tight grip, but she shook him off easily, and snapped out, "Not now!"

He dropped his hand and backed away from her.

Dwayne stepped so close to Annabelle the chill from his body made her shiver. "I want ten grand. You got way more for her than you said."

"I can do it again."

"Philip won't have anything to do with you. You're lucky he didn't kill you."

"Then you do it. Do you know the value of a dhampir? And they grow quickly. I can have two, three more before I call it quits."

His nose wrinkled in obvious disgust. "Just the money."

"That's a shame. Because you're not getting another dime. Now get out."

"I don't think so." He stepped forward, and finally, Annabelle felt terror.

# CHAPTER 34

An hour after he left Annabelle's, Dwayne returned to Blood Shots. He spoke to no one as he moved through the crowded bar and dance floor; he simply waved a distracted hand at anyone who called out his name in greeting. He beelined for the office, closed the door, and went straight to the computer. After logging in, he used the browser to open his banking information and verify the account had updated with the ten grand from Annabelle. He'd experienced a moment of regret after he'd forced it out of her, but they'd made him do it. Everything that happened to them was their own fault.

She had some nerve trying to stiff him. She'd received almost a hundred thousand for the girl. Stupid faeries were willing to pay anything for Philip's daughter. Who knew? Originally, the trio had expected a third that amount. When Dwayne learned exactly how much the couple had received and that they never updated him on those developments, he had to go after his fair share and punish them for cheating him.

That scheming bitch. Well, this time she'd ripped off the wrong guy, and he'd made her regret it. At least now he could pay down another portion of what he owed to Evans's crew. Soon, he'd be free of them all, and everything he made would be all his. Then he wouldn't have to dabble in all this illegal shit. Things would get back to normal between him and Philip, and his partner need never know Dwayne had ever veered from the straight and narrow.

Philip had insisted when the two went into business together that they detach themselves from any criminal connections, but Dwayne found staying clean more difficult than Philip had. For Dwayne, making money illegally had always come more easily than struggling to earn a living without breaking the law. Just why it mattered to Philip so much, Dwayne couldn't say for sure. He suspected it had to do with Philip's family. When he became a vampire, he'd disappeared from their lives, never turning even one of them, but his bloodline, the Belanger bloodline, remained his legacy.

That bloodline, as it turned out, was what the fae desired. It not only traced back to before the unmasquing, before Quebec, where the Belanger family lived, became Kébec, but it traced back to before the French settlers took it over. Philip Belanger had Métis roots. After the unmasquing, much of the land reverted to the descendants of the original inhabitants or ceded to hypernaturals. The Belangers gained from that, whereas most surviving humans lost everything.

Dwayne's family hadn't fared so well. The biggest stroke of luck he'd had was when he'd run into a vampire shortly after the unmasquing and she'd turned him. He'd asked for it—begged for it, if he were honest with himself. Those initial days became a nightmare blur because, while the vampire life agreed with him, the baby-vamp life almost destroyed his sanity.

He looked up, ready to give someone what for, when the door opened without an accompanying knock. He froze as Nicholas Sabatino strolled into the room.

"You're never supposed to come here," Dwayne said.

Evans's second in command sauntered to the bar and helped himself to two fingers of the best scotch, but Dwayne didn't stop him. While a human would never win against a vampire—or rarely, anyway—Dwayne knew better than to challenge the man. Whatever he wanted, odds were good Evans had sent him, and whatever Evans wanted, Dwayne would probably want to refuse. Yet until he paid off his debts to the syndicate, they owned him.

"Don't worry about it," Sabatino replied. "Belanger's not here. That's why I need your help."

"What's up?" But Dwayne had a horrible feeling he knew exactly what was up.

"Frank wants to know why Philip Belanger was found trespassing on fae land this morning. You were told to watch him."

Dwayne swallowed, trying to quell the rage that threatened to release his fangs. They had some nerve holding him accountable for what his partner did. "I alerted you he was searching for his daughter. That's as much as I knew. He never told me he'd found her."

"Well, he has, and he's causing problems for the fae. He's trespassing on their territory. We guaranteed them the girl was free and clear of family attachments, and then because you didn't stop him from pursuing her, we had to warn them he might show up. Imagine Frank's displeasure when Belanger actually made it that far."

Sabatino sprawled on the couch, draping his arm over the back of it, and sipped his drink. The scotch tempted Dwayne, and he went to the bar to pour one for himself. He kept his back to Sabatino, preferring to avoid the eye contact.

"What do you want me to do about it?"

"Belanger needs a reminder he can't renege on his promises."

Dwayne shrugged, still refusing to turn around and face the man. "So? That's what Evans has goons for."

"Not this time. This time, you're making the statement on his behalf."

Dwayne spun around because he understood now why Sabatino had come to him. "No. I'm almost paid up. I have another ten grand I can give you right now. That leaves fifty grand owing." He could take Annabelle up on her offer to give him a child. Or two. Two dhampirs, tops, and he could pay back everything he owed Evans and have money left over. Philip need never know of his involvement in any of this.

Sabatino shook his head, slowly, sadly. "But you're not paid up, so we won't argue about this. Evans wants you to do this one little thing for him. You do this, and he'll cancel half your remaining debt."

"Why me?" But he knew the answer. Evans wanted the syndicate left out of this. Sacrifice Dwayne's partnership with Philip, not Evans's. "He'd still know Evans was behind this. Who else would order this?"

"You would, my friend. You're the one who got this rolling."

He shook his head furiously. "No. Not me.

Annabelle. Marshall. All I did was nudge Philip in Annabelle's direction. I barely did anything."

"You got paid well for someone who barely did anything."

Dwayne pressed his lips together. How did they know? He'd never told them where he got the money he paid them. "You keeping tabs on me?"

"Wouldn't you, if someone owed you upwards of a hundred grand?"

In response, Dwayne sucked back half of the scotch in his glass.

Sabatino set his empty glass on the coffee table and stood. "I gotta go, but here's what you're gonna do." Sabatino stared into Dwayne's eyes without a trace of fear and outlined the plan.

"That'll destroy me. He'll never forgive me."

"Shame about that. Really." Sabatino rubbed his chin with his fingers as if contemplating the situation. "Frank feels horrible that you're in this situation. Tell you what. If Belanger holds it against you, we're willing to buy out your half of the bar. Help you cut ties and come out of it able to make a new start elsewhere."

So that was it. He takes the heat for whatever happens to the two humans, and when it all blows up in his face, he sells his half of the bar to Evans. "Philip won't have anything to do with the syndicate. You know that."

"My friend, it won't be his decision to make." He strode to the door and opened it wide. "Get moving. You have a lot of work to do."

Dwayne hung his head. He never saw the man leave, but he heard the door slam shut.

# CHAPTER 35

"How was school?" Kelsey asked Chase as he walked into the bookstore to start his shift. Exhausted, and relieved to see him, she wanted only to go upstairs and relax for the evening.

"Great. Divination exam today." He reached into the front pouch of his bag and pulled out a tarot deck. "Used this. Mind pulling a card? I want to see what you get."

Kelsey didn't like the idea of fortune telling. The Catholic Church only recently changed its stance on it being the devil's work, and it made her uneasy whenever Chase mentioned practicing it. But after all she'd been through, perhaps pulling a card to see what her future might hold would be a good thing.

"Sure. Let's see what you got."

He set his bag at his feet and removed the cards from their pack. He shuffled them and fanned them out. "Focus on a question you want answered and pick a card."

"Should I ask out loud?"

"If you want, but it's not necessary."

She inhaled deeply and let the breath out slowly. *What does my future hold?* She pulled a card and handed it, face down, to Chase.

He flipped it over. "The Fool."

"Is that good?"

He smiled. "Sure. It means new beginnings." He handed her the card.

She examined the picture, which showed a young man carrying a bag on a long stick, like a hobo. He walked so close to the edge of a cliff one misstep would send him hurtling over the edge. A white west highland terrier puppy bounded along in front of him. The young man had his gaze turned up to look at the sky, oblivious to where he stepped.

"It doesn't look good to me," she replied. "He's going to fall off that cliff. Does this mean I'm not watching where I'm going?"

"It might if it were reversed, but when you handed it to me, it was right-side up. In that case, it means someone starting a new journey. It's a fresh start or a new adventure."

"Oh." She contemplated. "Well, I haven't had this bookstore for long. I suppose this is my new beginning."

"Could be. But it could be something else coming up on the horizon. This card doesn't represent your past. It also signifies a leap of faith."

"Are you sure it's not my past? I took a leap of faith when I left Blair." She smiled, but inside the doubt had her heart pounding. After all, she'd asked about her future, not her past or her present. "That was interesting. Thanks." She handed him back the card and sighed, feeling wearier than she had when he'd first walked in. "I'm beat. When you've put your stuff away, I'm heading upstairs to get dinner started before Josh gets home from work."

She looked forward to their first quiet evening together since Dakota had disappeared. Kelsey bit her lip at the thought of Dakota, but if the vampire couldn't rescue her, what could anyone expect a couple of humans to do? *I have nothing to feel guilty about. We tried.*

"No worries." Chase's tone was light, happy, and he beamed a smile at her. How Kelsey envied his carefree life. The young man had only his schoolwork and his job to worry about. He'd mentioned a girlfriend but didn't discuss the relationship with his boss. As far as Kelsey knew, things were fine for him on that front. She didn't know much about his family, either, but since he never complained about them, she assumed all was well.

"Thanks." She waited for him while he went to the staff room, and when he returned and assumed his position behind the counter, she gave the store a once-over.

A couple sat at one of the tables drinking lattes. Three other customers browsed the bookshelves. Mondays were typically slow. Chase should have a quiet enough evening. He might even manage to get some studying done.

"Have a good night." She brushed past him as he responded in kind, and left through the back of the store.

As she climbed the steps to her apartment, she mentally reviewed the contents of her fridge and cupboards for dinner ideas. She should've thought ahead. Now they'd have to have something from a can or something simple she could throw together.

She unlocked the door at the top of the stairs and stepped into her living room. After locking the door again, she set her cell phone down on the desk and headed for the bathroom to wash her hands. She almost made it as far as the hallway when a figure stepped from the shadows of her bedroom.

Her heart thudded in her chest; her pulse thundered in her ears. Kelsey gasped, but before she could retreat, the figure stepped all the way into the hall and she recognized him.

"Dwayne." Her respiration slowed, and her pulse quieted to almost normal. With a start, she realized he must be here about Philip. Her brow wrinkled and she bit her lip. What if something had happened to him?

"What's wrong? What happened? Is it Philip?"

When Dwayne didn't respond, she twisted her hands together, and panic flooded her voice. "Where's Philip? Did he return?"

Dwayne met her gaze, his mouth turned down. "I'm sorry."

"Did he find Dakota?"

He gave her a slight nod.

"Oh." All her relief flooded into that one word. *Thank God.* "Did he bring her back? Is she with him? Where are they?" She couldn't stop the questions from tumbling out, but as it dawned on her he wasn't responding to any of them, the hair lifted on the back of her neck and she shivered. "What's wrong?"

Maybe it wasn't Philip. Or Dakota. "Did something happen?" What if it was Josh? She whirled around to go for her cell phone and call him, but Dwayne was on her before she could take a single step.

He grabbed her by the arm and pulled her tight into

his body. "We'll have none of that. Do as I say and you'll be fine."

She started to cry out, but Dwayne covered her mouth with his hand and hissed at her. "Shh. Not a sound," he whispered in her ear.

From the direction of the kitchen came the sound of a key turning in the door to the backyard. Josh was home.

*** 

Josh whistled a merry tune as he sauntered into the kitchen, dropped his backpack on a chair, and grabbed a cola from the fridge. He popped the tab and took a deep swallow, thirsty from his walk home from the subway. The apartment was quiet, so he assumed his mother was still down in the store.

*Should've stuck my head in, told her I was home.* She'd have immediately dropped everything and joined him up here to make dinner. He smiled affectionately at the idea. Perhaps he should surprise her and get dinner started before she got here. He almost laughed out loud at the idea of shocking her. Plus, if they ate early, he could meet up with Anthony for a while before he had to get to bed. His first day on the job had tired him. Who knew cataloging objects in the museum could be so exhausting?

A noise from the living room caught his attention, and half thinking his mother had walked in without him hearing her, he strolled toward the sound.

"Hey, Mom, I was thinking I could—"

A vampire who looked familiar blocked the living room's entrance. Confused, Josh looked past the intruder, searching for any sign of Kelsey. He spotted her cell phone on the desk and knew for certain she was home.

"Who are you? Why are you here?"

The vampire frowned. "He erased your memory?" He shook his head. "Doesn't matter."

"Where's my mother?" A name popped into Josh's head, but he didn't know how he knew it. "Dwayne."

"Busy." Dwayne stared into Josh's eyes, so he quickly averted his gaze, afraid the vampire intended to hypnotize him.

"Relax, kid. I'm not the one you need to worry about."

"Really? Who do I need to worry about?"

"Your vampire buddy. Seems he didn't keep his promise to some very dangerous people."

Josh gulped. "What vampire buddy? Where's my mother?"

"Safe. For now."

"Where? Prove it."

"You'll just have to trust me on it."

Josh shuffled a step toward the desk where Kelsey's phone rested. It was a long shot, but if he could grab it without Dwayne spotting him, he could call emergency. The cops would descend on the place, and in the confusion, the vampire might slip away. Or kill them both—unless his mother was elsewhere—but he couldn't just do nothing. If Dwayne held his mother somewhere, it was up to Josh to save them.

"Don't take another step." One moment, Dwayne stood on the other side of the room, the next, he was in Josh's face with a tight grip on his upper arm. "We're taking a little trip, and you're going to cooperate."

"Why would I do that?" But he knew. The vampire would use his mother as leverage.

Verifying Josh's fears, Dwayne said, "Your mother will die if you don't do exactly as I say."

"I want to see her."

"Oh, don't worry. You will," Dwayne replied, sending a chill down Josh's spine.

Refusing to show weakness, he said, "Then take me to her."

Dwayne sneered. "You can try to hide it, son, but you reek of fear."

Josh drew himself up to his full five-foot-eleven height, thrust out his chin, and puffed out his chest. "Of course I'm afraid. You're a vampire. I'm not stupid. But if you think I won't fight you, you're wrong."

"Your mommy would be proud." The vampire bared his fangs. "Right until the moment I bite down on her neck."

With a cry of rage, Josh attacked, aiming a kick at Dwayne's knees, hoping it would disable him enough to allow a chance to escape. It didn't work. The vampire laughed, and with casual slowness, cold-cocked the boy. The room spun and then faded as he was tossed over the vampire's shoulder.

# CHAPTER 36

The fae could die, but that didn't mean Philip wanted them dead. His mission here was to rescue Dakota, not trigger an international incident with the Interspecies World Consortium, Earth's governing body. It had formed after the interspecies wars resulting from the unmasquing. All species had to keep the peace. A vampire entering fae territory and attacking and killing numerous inhabitants in that realm would attract more than local constabulary attention. It might not escalate to international levels, but Philip didn't want to risk even national attention. Instead of killing the guards, he incapacitated them and locked them in their own cells.

When he was done, he studied his handiwork and listened for the approach of any more guards. All was quiet except for the raspy breaths of the caged faeries.

"Sorry, darlings. If you'll excuse me, I've got business with the prince." He scooped his cowboy hat, which had fallen off his head in the melee, from the ground and bowed to the prisoners. He took quick stock of his surroundings and determined which way they'd brought him when they entered the prison area. It was underground, so upward was the way to go.

He easily backtracked to the entrance but had to pause to knock out the guards there and cuff them together. From there, he turned his back on the outer door and veered down a passageway that took him farther into the castle's interior. They likely held Dakota close to the prince, and Philip followed the opulence. The richer and more elaborate the decor in the hallways became, the more certain he was that he followed the correct path.

While he walked, he kept to the shadows, hiding in nooks or empty rooms as servants came and went about their business. No one noticed him, and after a while, that fact unsettled him. This was too easy, but if they'd set a trap for him, all he could do was spring it and deal with it.

He opened doors, peered into alcoves. When he found a locked door, he kicked it in. Unless they planned to cut off his head or stake him through the heart, he could easily fight off anyone who confronted him. Perhaps they understood that and so they stayed out of his way. Silver bullets would slow him down, of course, but the fae weren't known for using guns. Silver-tipped arrows would be more their style, so he moved cautiously and methodically forward.

The farther he walked without opposition, the more uneasy he grew. He hadn't even seen a servant recently. When he reached a set of large double doors, he froze. He'd picked up a scent that had infused Dakota's bedroom when he'd searched it. She was in there. His daughter. The young woman he'd never met but who meant so much to him he'd risk an international incident to save her. Philip tried the door handles, and they turned easily. He thrust open the doors but remained in the hallway.

Dakota and the prince were the sole occupants of the room, an enormous library with floor-to-ceiling bookcases on almost every wall. One wall featured a massive brick fireplace, and a roaring fire blazed in the hearth, taking the castle's natural chill from the air. In front of the fireplace, Culain sat at one end of a couch while Dakota sat at the other. On the coffee table before them rested a service for two with coffee, tea, pastries, fruit, and milk and sugar.

*How quaint.*

Dakota jumped to her feet, but Culain waved her down, and to Philip's annoyance, she sat.

He ignored the fae prince and spoke to Dakota. "Don't sit. You're coming with me. Now." His annoyance turned to fury when she remained silent and seated, and she looked at Culain for guidance.

"You're trespassing," Culain said, "and if you don't leave now, I'll have you charged under the Species Cooperation Act."

Disregarding the threat, Philip scanned the area for traps and then stepped into the room. "She's my daughter. You kidnapped her. She decides whether to stay or go." He strode to Dakota's side and held out his hand. "Come."

His child hung her head and then shook it. "I'm staying."

Philip lifted his chin, glared at Culain, and opened his mouth to show his fangs. "What have you done to her?" He crouched at her side in time to brush away a tear as it slid down her cheek.

"I've done nothing. She's chosen to stay and fulfill

the obligations of her contract."

"Not her contract," Philip said. "Her mother signed that contract."

"Her mother, who had sole custody, and my parents, who made the arrangement for me." Culain stood. "It's a legitimate, binding agreement in which you play no part."

"Dakota can speak for herself."

"Philip ... Father." She took his hands in hers. "I've decided to stay."

"Are they forcing you?" When she hesitated, he turned to Culain. "You're coercing her. I don't care how you're doing it, or what you think you can do about it, but we're leaving together. Now."

Footsteps approached from the direction Philip had come, and when he looked up to see who'd arrived, his eyes went wide and he jumped to his feet. Dwayne stepped into the room, and he dragged Joshua Davis in with him. The kid had a black eye, and Philip's surge of rage returned. If his partner had done that, he'd answer to Philip for it. And where was Kelsey?

Dakota cried out and also leaped to standing. Philip was gratified to see she ignored Culain's sharp directive to sit back down. She raced to Josh's side and threw her arms around him. He wrapped one arm around her—Dwayne retained a solid grip on the kid's other arm—and Dakota sobbed into his shoulder.

Josh's eyes grew wide and his jaw dropped when he recognized Dakota, and while he kept his arm around her, his expression remained one of stunned shock. "Dakota?" He kissed her hair, which got a rise out of Culain.

"Dakota," the prince said, echoing Josh, but with a commanding rather than questioning tone.

"How are you here?" Josh asked. Wonder and fear filled his voice, and his terrified gaze met Philip's stony one.

"How are *you* here?" Philip responded, but he pinned his gaze on Dwayne, and his voice held neither wonder nor fear, but fury.

"He's with me," Dwayne said. "A mutual acquaintance wanted us to deliver a message. You ought to know who and what I mean. Give it up, Belanger. You're done. Go home before it's too late."

"He's got my mom," Josh shouted before Philip could respond. "He'll hurt her."

Philip swallowed. Served him right for leaving Josh and Kelsey unguarded. He hoped Dwayne was here to alert him to the danger, but something about his partner's demeanor told him that wasn't the case.

"Who has her, Josh?"

"Dwayne. She's locked in the trunk of his car."

Philip's hands clenched and unclenched, and his nostrils flared. He bared his teeth, exposing his fangs again. "What the hell's she doing there?"

"Easy, partner." Dwayne's body went rigid, and he raised a palm in a placating gesture. "You're lucky it's me they told to handle this."

Philip doubted it. For the moment, he let it go. But as soon as they were out of here—with Dakota—he and his partner would have a long chat with the truth as the main attraction.

Culain moved swiftly to Dakota and extricated her from Josh's arm. Her breath hitched, but she let him do it even though Josh tried to keep her near him. She pulled away, shaking her head.

"I'm staying," she said. "It'll be fine. I want to be here."

"You're clearly upset," Josh said. "You're not fine. It won't be fine. They're making you do this." He glared at Culain. "He's making you say that. What are you doing here? I thought you were visiting your dad?"

"Where would you get that idea?"

"You. Didn't you tell me …" He scrubbed his hands over his face and rubbed his temples as if he had a headache.

*Shit.* Once the truth started to come out, the kid would remember it all, including Philip hypnotizing him. If Josh directed his anger in Philip's direction, that would be fine, but when his memory fully returned, Josh would remember Kelsey gave permission for this. He'd be furious with her. Since more important things needed his attention, Philip pushed that problem aside for the moment and turned to Culain.

"We're leaving. With Dakota. You report me, I'll report you for kidnapping. For trafficking."

"No one will believe you when they see the signed documents. Arranged marriages are part of our culture. They're legal."

Philip gritted his teeth and almost cut his own lips on his fangs. "They're not part of our culture."

"They are if all parties agree to it."

Philip rolled his eyes and huffed out an exasperated breath. "Dakota never agreed. She signed nothing."

"Father …"

When she didn't continue, he knew. "Damn it. You signed. He made you sign, didn't he?"

She shook her head. "I signed, but he didn't make me. We made a deal."

# CHAPTER 37

If it shocked her when her father had burst into the room, it unhinged her when Josh appeared. Dakota used all the will she could muster to hide her pain. The tears flowed while the young man held her, but when they drew apart, she dried her eyes and pasted on a stoic front. Perhaps someday, her father and Josh would understand. She refused to dwell on the day when she learned Josh had found someone else, but she hoped he eventually would. It would mean he'd survived this ordeal. She needed to do this. For their safety, for the safety of others—and for the power she'd have when she became queen.

She'd never wanted power before—never craved it, never thought about it. That all changed during her conversation with Culain after lunch. Now, she wanted it with all her being, and she planned to never look back.

"Yes, Father, I signed the agreement." When Philip's face darkened, she took Culain's hand and gave him what she hoped was a look of affection.

To her surprise, Philip's shoulders dropped and his features smoothed out. He turned imploring eyes on her. "Can't you call me Dad? Father makes me sound like a priest."

She giggled at the priest comment but cut the laugh short with a surge of annoyance. Giggling like a schoolgirl. Not queenly behavior. She contemplated his request.

"Dad?" She'd never thought of him as Dad. She'd never known him during her formative years, but she'd known of him. When he burst through those doors, she held no feelings of love for him. To her, he was a stranger, but given their blood relationship, calling him Philip or Mr. Belanger seemed too reserved, too formal. Father had seemed a decent compromise.

"I wasn't a part of your life, but if you stay here, maybe I could visit." He glanced at Culain and then returned his focus to Dakota. "If you must marry this faerie, perhaps they'd allow me to see you sometimes. I can come across the veil and return with no consequences. If they agree to that, I'll leave. I'll drop the whole thing and let you stay."

Josh cried out, his anguished "no" rending the air. Dakota gave her boyfriend—potential boyfriend, the one that got away—an aggrieved look, and replied, "We could arrange that; I'm sure." When she looked into Culain's eyes, she did so with a confidence and determination that told him he had to agree even if she'd already signed the document.

He gave a slight nod. "We could make arrangements to allow it." He sounded less sure than she had, but she accepted it. If the other fae didn't like the intrusion into their realm, they should have kidnapped someone more malleable. She'd play their game, until the game became hers to direct.

Culain, staring at the doorway, suddenly relaxed, a look of relief crossing his face. Following his gaze, Dakota heard the approaching tread of heavy boots in the hallway. Both vampires and the one human spun around to face whoever appeared.

"You were watched from the moment you stepped foot in here. All of you. It's by my grace you got this far," Culain said. "You wanted to see your daughter, Philip, and you have. She's made clear to you she's staying. The guards will escort you out."

Philip approached Dakota and held out his arms to her. She hesitantly met him, halfway between Josh and Culain. The guards streamed into the room then—four of them—and she smiled at the audacity of the fae believing they could restrain vampires with four measly guards. She hugged her father, and as they held one another, she whispered, "Go with them. Look after Josh for me."

"I promise." He squeezed her tight. "I've always cared for you, my darling. This prince gives you any problems, you get a message to me. Deal?"

"Deal." She could promise that because as long as Philip and Josh remained safe, she'd play the role the fae had cast her in. In time, she might even come to care for Culain—so long as he was the man she believed him to be.

They drew apart at the same time, and Philip held her at arm's length for a moment, his dark brown eyes staring into hers. For a second, she felt the pull of his vampire powers and almost lost herself in his gaze. Then her own abilities asserted themselves, and she broke the connection as if it had never formed.

"Goodbye, Father." She glanced at Culain and then

back to Philip. He opened his mouth, and she knew he meant to argue against her words, so she amended them. "Goodbye for now—Dad."

Another anguished cry escaped Josh. She moved to him and offered him her hand. He took it, but when he tried to pull her in for a hug, she shook her head.

"Friends," she said. "Never more than that, but always that." If she hugged him, she might take it all back and damn them all. So she straightened her back, pulling herself up to her full height, and gave him a regret-filled smile.

"Dakota …" His voice cracked as he said her name, and it broke her heart, but now wasn't the time to grieve. She'd do that later, in private.

"Surely you didn't think what we were to one another was more than friendship." She hated to gaslight him. They'd had a mutual attraction. They'd both expected to take their relationship to the next level, but now, she had to break his heart and force him to believe he'd imagined the whole thing.

He scowled, and then his expression grew pained. "I know what we had. I know what we could have."

"Friends," she insisted. "But I have obligations now. We can't see each other anymore, but we'll always remain friends. If you ever need anything I can help with, if it's within my power, I'll help you." With her free hand, she touched his cheek delicately, savoring the roughness of his skin, letting the stubble tickle the pads of her fingers.

"Sure." His voice was even, controlled, but she couldn't tell if he controlled anger or grief. Probably both. He shook her hand, squeezed it, and let it drop.

"Let's go." Josh directed that at Philip. "My mother needs your help." He tossed a hate-filled glare at

Dwayne. Before he spun on his heel and headed for the doors, Josh gave Dakota one last longing look. "Goodbye." In an echo of her words to her father, he added, "For now."

Her gaze followed Josh to the doors, and she remained standing there, staring, even after the vampires and the faerie escort had disappeared after him. They'd shut the doors behind them, and though she listened for the sound of the lock snicking into place, it never came. She didn't assume that meant they trusted her. Perhaps they concluded she'd lost the will to fight them.

They were wrong. If it took her years of play-acting, years of going along, eventually, they'd learn Dakota Lawson never gave up.

*** 

Josh trudged along behind the vampires and two of the guards, while the other two guards trailed after him. The return trip to the mushroom ring barely registered, as it had barely registered coming in, but for different reasons. On the way in, rescuing Dakota and getting his mother back preoccupied him. On the return trip, grief and loss—and getting his mother back— preoccupied him.

When they emerged from the ring, they left their fae escort behind. Philip and Dwayne had argued over who should lead and who should follow, and in the spirit of getting the hell away from the crazy vamps and moving this circus along, Josh brushed past them and stepped through the veil.

"Hurry up!" He resented every extra second his mother had to spend curled up in the trunk of

Dwayne's car. Without waiting for his companions, he picked his way down the trail that led from the forest. As he expected they would, the two vampires caught up to him almost instantly.

The bickering picked up where it had left off, each man speaking as though he held the moral high ground.

"Why are you playing lackey for Evans?" Philip began.

"Sabatino, more like," Dwayne replied. "And you're lucky I ran interference, so you're welcome."

"You expect me to be grateful? You stuffed Kelsey in the trunk of your car."

"She's fine. It's night, so no sun to heat up the vehicle. I had to put her somewhere. It was the safest place I could think of."

"You're a real humanitarian." But his voice had lost most of its fury.

The trail ended, and the trio stepped out of the trees and onto the side of the dirt road. Dwayne's car, a Lexus, stood on their left.

Josh rushed to it. "I'm here, Mom. You all right?"

When he got no response, he hollered, "Open the trunk, you son of a bitch. Something's wrong."

Dwayne held up his remote, and the locks snapped open when he pressed the button. Philip beat Josh to the vehicle's back end and threw open the lid. All three peered into the trunk, Josh preparing to dive in and pull his mother out.

It was empty.

# CHAPTER 38

Josh broke the stunned silence with a panicked cry. "Where is she?"

Philip put a hand on the boy's arm to rein him in before he jumped Dwayne, which wouldn't help anything.

"I thought you said you left her in the trunk." Philip leveled his gaze on his partner but kept his voice calm. No need to freak the kid out any more than he already was. There had to be a logical explanation.

"I told you the truth. She was here when we left." Dwayne tilted his head at Josh. "He gave me a hard time about it, but it was risky enough taking one human in to see the fae. Plus, I needed the insurance."

*The hostage, you mean.* But Philip kept that unhelpful statement to himself as well. The conversation he'd have with his partner when Josh and Kelsey were safe at home would be epic, but for now, they had to focus on finding out what the hell had happened to Kelsey.

*Merde. What a mess.*

Philip peered into the trunk. Perhaps Kelsey had

freed herself.

"I disabled the release. I'm not stupid," Dwayne said.

Which meant he'd planned this out. Another point they'd have to discuss later.

"Besides," Dwayne added, "she was tied up."

Josh glared at Dwayne as he said that, alerting Philip to yet one more bone of contention between Philip's partner and the boy. Dwayne would have a lot to answer for when they resolved all this.

"The fae?" Philip wondered.

Dwayne shrugged, but then slowly shook his head and pursed his lips. With a wary glance at Josh, he said, "Unlikely."

"What's likely, then?"

Josh broke into the discussion. "Evans. Or that other guy who works for Evans. They got her while we went after Dakota. You left her here for them like an offering." He lunged at Dwayne, grabbing the vampire by the lapel, but only because Dwayne tolerated the attack. If he'd wanted to dodge the boy, he'd have easily done so.

He extricated Josh's fingers from his dress shirt, brushing imaginary dirt off with exaggerated swipes. "Control yourself. I can't think if I have to swat at you, you little gnat."

Josh squinched his eyes and sneered. He remained silent, and his hands dropped to his sides but they remained fisted.

"Why would Evans have her?" Philip took a step toward Dwayne but stopped short of crowding him.

"You have to ask?" Dwayne tsked. "You brought this on her." He waved a hand at Josh and Philip. "Both of you. Kelsey is culpable as well. You didn't drop your hunt for Dakota, but you told them you would. What did you expect to happen? You think word wouldn't get out?" He turned on his heel and paced the road's gravel shoulder in the deepening dusk.

"Christ. They came to me at the bar." He halted and spun around to face Philip. "They've got me by the balls, and I have to go along with whatever they tell me to do." As soon as he stopped talking, a look of horror crossed his face.

"Interesting. Why is that?"

Resignation replaced horror. "I might as well tell you; Evans is buying out my share of the bar."

"Never mind that!" Josh said. "How do we get my mom back?"

Philip spared the boy a sympathetic glance before focusing on Dwayne once more. "He's right. We'll discuss this, but not now. How do we find Kelsey? Does she have her phone?"

As if in answer to the question, his phone sounded with Kelsey's ringtone. He snatched it from the holster at his waist and answered it on the second ring. "Kelsey?"

"Not exactly."

Philip recognized the voice. Quickly, he went through the motions to record the call.

"Nicholas Sabatino. How are you?" He injected mockery into the question. "Things going pretty well for you these days? I sure hope nothing turns your good fortune."

"Quit the posturing, Belanger. We both know I've got the leverage here."

"Maybe. Maybe not."

In a wary voice, Sabatino replied, "What's that mean?"

"It means," Philip said, speaking slowly and enunciating each word while simultaneously wrapping an arm around Josh and clapping a hand over the boy's mouth, "you assume I give a shit what happens to her."

Josh struggled against the vampire, and when it was obvious the hand wasn't going anywhere, he bit down on it. Philip ignored the pain and tightened his grip on Josh.

"The boy cares."

"What makes you think I give a shit about that?" As he spoke, he threw a dirty look in Dwayne's direction. He looked way too complacent for the betrayals he'd perpetrated. Philip likely knew only a small part of Dwayne's dirty dealings. He couldn't wait to learn the whole story and make his partner pay.

"Do you give a shit about your worthless hide?"

"You threatening me? Because Evans and I have an understanding." Though it was possible Evans no longer thought so.

"About that. Frank says to tell you you're even. Behave, and we won't kill the woman. But you and Frank are done."

Well, he'd wanted to sever ties with the mobster but hadn't figured out how. He'd have to thank Dwayne for mixing things up with Evans and his crew to the point where they wanted to part ways now. Then why did he suddenly feel like he was on the losing end of a bad deal? He balked, to test Sabatino's response.

"No deal."

Josh, who'd gone limp tucked under Philip's arm, struggled again, grunting and trying to shout through the hand over his mouth. He also went to his go-to move of chomping down on the vampire's hand.

Philip pressed his lips to Josh's ear. "Trust me and

shut up." Josh settled down, and Philip whispered, "Stay out of it."

The silence on the other end of the phone had drawn out a while, Sabatino perhaps keeping quiet to try to catch any conversation on Philip's end. He waited the mobster out.

Finally, Sabatino broke the silence. "Then she's as good as dead."

"What does that get you?" Philip kept his voice detached. Cold. "Just out of curiosity. You think the boy won't go to the authorities?"

"What if he does?" Sabatino laughed. "They'll care as much as you do." He raised his voice. "They'll never tie it to us. Your word means nothing in a courtroom."

"His word and the recording I'm making might do the trick, though. Isn't that right, Nicholas Sabatino?" He used the mobster's name to remind him this wasn't the first time in the conversation he'd been identified.

An audible intake of breath came through the cell phone.

Philip continued. "You'll let her go, and you'll let the kid go. Tell your boss my daughter remains in her new home, and I'm not pursuing the matter further. No blowback. Anything else we need to discuss is between me and Evans." He glared at Dwayne. "And Dwayne Rathburn. Tell me where to pick up Kelsey. It'll be in everyone's best interests to have her home safe and sound. Are we in agreement?"

"She'll be in the café." The line went dead.

"Let's go." Philip released Josh, who raced to the car and hopped into the back seat.

Dwayne started to move toward the driver's side, but Philip stopped him. "I don't know what you did, but if something happens to either of those two humans, I'll hold you responsible."

"I tried to keep them safe. Whatever happens to them is on you, not me. They're in this because of you."

"I know what's my fault. I also know Sabatino went to the bar and suddenly you had Josh and the mob has Kelsey." The two glared at each other until Philip, through gritted teeth, said, "Get in the car."

With a silent shrug, Dwayne did as ordered.

# CHAPTER 39

Kelsey tested the rope binding her hands behind her to the chair on which she sat, but her struggles only managed to deepen the rope burns on her wrists. Each ankle was also bound to the chair, but she focused on getting her hands free.

The lights in the café were off, the only illumination coming from streetlights and a full moon shining in through the windows. It gave the place a creepy, haunted feel. Perhaps it was haunted. She'd heard more ghosts traversed the veil since the unmasquing though she had no personal experience to verify it.

The thugs who'd taken her from Dwayne's car positioned her chair facing the store's entrance. They said nothing to her, and she had stopped trying to reason with them long ago. She'd hoped the fact they visited her every month for coffee and protection money would count for something, but the only reward her attempts at conversation with them got her was a backhand across the face. Her stubborn streak meant she'd made four tries at talking to them before she decided the effort wasn't worth the punishment.

Currently, the three men who held her hid in various parts of the store. Sabatino took up a position directly behind his captive. She couldn't see if he still held his gun, but it was no longer pressed to her head, so she considered that a win.

She'd eavesdropped on his end of the conversation with Philip, her blood boiling as she understood he cared little about what happened to her or to Josh.

*Why would he? He's a vampire.* They lacked humanity. A conscience. She'd fooled herself into thinking he might be different because he'd wanted to save his daughter, but that was out of ego. He probably considered the girl property, and when her mother sold her, he'd considered her stolen property. *Wounded ego. He doesn't care about anyone but himself.*

Dwayne was just as bad. He'd done Sabatino's dirty work, and now here she was, bait for the vampires. The worst part of it was they'd bring Josh along and then Evans and his mob would have her son too. That thought had her struggling against the ropes again until the pain became unbearable and blood trickled down her fingers.

The door blew open, and she had a moment of rage that the vampire had broken the lock and now she'd have to call a locksmith, when she spotted the two thugs unconscious on the floor. Dwayne and Philip stood, one beside each body.

Sabatino opened the conversation. "I've got a gun trained on her head."

The barrel poked the back of her skull once more and she closed her eyes.

"One move and I'll blow her brains out. The bullets are silver. If I hit either of you with one, you'll feel it."

"Did you think we wouldn't smell the trap? And your blood, Sabatino?"

"Did you think I wouldn't have two more men watching for the boy?" the mobster replied. "They already have him."

"Where's Josh?" Kelsey cut in, her eyes springing open. Nothing else mattered to her. Not the stupid lock on the door, not the vampires, and not Dakota—and where the hell was Dakota? She hoped the dhampir girl was with Josh. With her vampire-like powers, she'd be a help if Sabatino's men showed up.

"We didn't bring him," Philip replied. "He's safe."

"He'll be here shortly," Sabatino said. "Just received a text from one of my guys. Thank you for the intel, Dwayne."

Kelsey cried out in anguish while Philip snarled and turned on Dwayne. "You messaged them? You told them where we left the boy?"

Dwayne stepped back and pulled a gun on Philip. "Sorry. Had to. They gave me no choice. I gotta look out for my own interests. Besides, you said you didn't care what happened to them."

Philip didn't reply to that, but he didn't have to. His lack of response told them all he'd lied, bluffing to try to save mother and son.

"I'll kill you for this." Philip turned his steely gaze from Dwayne to Sabatino.

"Did you think there'd be no blowback for lying to Frank Evans?" Sabatino said. "You gave your word, and you broke your word."

"We're even then because you said you'd release both of them. I left Dakota with the faeries."

"Yet you went after her when we told you not to. I don't enjoy my customers complaining to me. They're promised anonymity. It's part of the service we offer."

"The service you're offering is illegal. Evans knows I want no part in his illegal activities. He promised to keep me clear of them."

"This had nothing to do with you."

"Dakota is my daughter. This had everything to do with me."

A commotion at the door made them all turn in that direction. Two men walked in, Josh stumbling into the store between them. When he spotted Kelsey tied to the chair, he gave a shout and ran to her side.

"Mom, you okay?" He threw his arms around her.

"You can go now, Dwayne. None of this concerns you anymore," Sabatino said.

"You son of a bitch." Philip made a grab for his partner, but the two men who'd brought Josh in raised their weapons.

"Their bullets are silver as well," Sabatino said. "Go ahead, Belanger, test them."

Philip dropped his arms to his sides, but drew his lips back, his fangs flashing white in the lights from the street.

A groan from the floor signaled the two men Dwayne and Philip had knocked out were coming to. Dwayne gave them a hand up. "Sorry, boys. Tried to be gentle."

They scowled at him but remained silent.

"Well." Dwayne stepped toward the door. "I need to book. Got packing to do. We'll probably not meet again." His gaze landed on Kelsey. "Sorry for your troubles. You shouldn't have gotten involved with this guy." He tilted his head in Philip's direction. "Nothing but trouble." He laughed and was gone.

"What does he want?" Philip tipped a chin at Kelsey

and Josh. "For their freedom."

"Nothing." Sabatino stroked a hand over Kelsey's hair, and she wriggled out from under it by jerking forward.

"Don't touch me."

Philip stepped toward them, and Sabatino and all four of his goons aimed their weapons at him.

"Not another step."

"Then let them go. I'll go with you to Evans's, and we'll sort all this out with him."

"That's not the plan."

Philip bared his fangs again and snarled. "Then what is?"

"You all owe a debt to Frank. If you want to clear it, you'll have to work it off."

"Evans and I are done."

"Suit yourself." Sabatino turned the gun on Josh and shot him in the gut.

Kelsey screamed, an anguished, blood-curdling cry.

Philip moved lightning fast. In a whirl, the four thugs were on the ground, and Sabatino had a bullet through his brain.

"Call 9-1-1," Kelsey screamed. "Oh, God, Josh. Please don't die." She strained against the ropes. "Help him."

Philip ripped off his shirt, kneeled beside Josh, and cradled the boy in his arms. He pressed the shirt to the wound, but almost instantly, it soaked with blood.

"What are you doing? Call for help!"

Blood trickled from Kelsey's raw-scraped wrists, but she ignored that and the pain, and continued to wriggle and struggle to work free the knots.

Philip gazed at her with sorrow, and she heard her son whisper, "I'm so cold."

"They won't get here in time," Philip said.

She whimpered. "Please, do something."

"Kelsey, there's only one thing I can do." He bared his fangs.

"Oh, God." He meant turn Josh. Turn her boy into one of them. A monster.

"He's damaged internally and losing too much blood too quickly. If I don't bite him and then feed him my blood, he'll die."

But if she gave him permission to do that, her son would lose his soul. She stared at his sheet-white face. His closed eyes. "No, take him to the hospital. You can get there in seconds. They'll save him."

"They can't. Don't you understand? I can smell death on him." Philip's voice was gentle but urgent. "You have seconds left, and then even I can't save him. What do you want me to do?"

He was leaving it up to her. He could've acted on his own, but he left the decision to her because she was Josh's mother. Would a monster do that?

"Oh, God." But this didn't involve God. God hadn't stopped Sabatino from pulling the trigger. The only one here to save Josh, to save her, was the monster God had brought into their lives. Life or death. Time was running out.

She met Philip's gaze and in a firm, steady voice said, "Do it."

# CHAPTER 40

Tears streamed down Kelsey's face as Philip leaned down to her son's neck and bit gently into it. She kept her gaze trained on the scene, refusing to permit herself the luxury of turning away. Whatever her son endured, whatever happened to him, she'd bear witness.

As the vampire fed, Josh's eyes snapped open, but they were glazed and unseeing. He moaned, and Kelsey sobbed and cried out when the moan sounded closer to pleasure than pain. She wanted to change her mind then, to tell the vampire to stop, please stop. She opened her mouth to do just that, but nothing came out except a strangled cry.

Her wide, horrified eyes remained fixed on the scene. Her ears strained to hear any small sound. To witness. To participate.

Philip raised his free arm to his mouth and gashed the wrist with his fangs. He held the wound to Josh's mouth and spoke gently. "Drink, my son."

Josh's lips rooted, latched on, and suckled, like a

babe nuzzling his mother's nipple. He fed eagerly, lustfully, making contented, delighted sounds as he did.

The bile rose in Kelsey's throat, and she forced it down.

*Oh, God, Josh, what have I done? Oh, my baby.* Her sobs grew louder, more anguished, until Philip drew his wrist away from Josh's mouth and whispered, "Enough, Josh. You've had enough."

Her son struggled and clamped a hand on the vampire's forearm to drag the wrist back to his greedy mouth. "More. I'm so hungry." His eyes opened wide, and when his gaze landed on his mother, he hissed and fangs sprang from his gums. He leaped to his feet and lunged at her, but Philip restrained him.

"No, not her. I'll teach you to control it, but for now …" Philip led the boy to one of the unconscious goons.

"Eat. But not too much."

The boy fell on the man, and Kelsey heard a crunch as her son used his new fangs for the first time.

This too she witnessed, and though she thought she'd cried out all the tears she had in her, she was wrong. More sobs wrenched from deep inside, hard and fast and painful. Her body arched against the restraints.

She felt Philip's hands working her free of the ropes before she realized he'd reached her side.

"I'll have to keep him with me. He can't be alone with you, and he can't go anywhere alone." Philip's tone was apologetic.

"Why didn't you stop them before they shot my boy? You let him shoot my baby." Her legs were free, but her wrists were still bound, and she forced herself to hold still while he worked the knots.

"I'm sorry. I waited too long. I never meant for this to happen. I was afraid if I moved, he'd shoot one of us. I needed a distraction. When he shot Josh, that was it, but it certainly wasn't the distraction I wanted."

The ropes fell from her wrists, and Philip instantly went to Josh's side. He pulled the feasting boy away from the unconscious man.

Josh, blood no longer pouring from his now-healed gut, struggled to return to his meal. Philip held him tight and rocked him in his arms.

"Shh. It's good now. You've had enough." His voice was gentle, soothing.

The bile rose again in Kelsey's throat, and, once again, she quashed it. "You killed Sabatino. Evans's men will tell him what happened." Hope left her and despair filled the void. "What can we do?"

She'd lose everything she'd worked so hard for: her store, her home, maybe her son. Probably her life. Kelsey kneeled beside Josh and tried to take him in her arms, but Philip knocked her aside as Josh grabbed for her.

"No," Philip said. "He won't care you're his mother. He'll tear you apart the same as he'd tear apart a stranger right now."

She choked on another sob, and then, with an effort of will, shut down the tears. No more grief. No regrets. Her son lived. Or, rather, he wasn't dead. *He's undead.*

"What can we do?" she asked.

"We've got to disappear."

"Where? I've got nowhere to go." She gazed pointedly at Josh. "We've got nowhere to go. I won't leave him."

"I'll take care of you, both of you, but you must trust me." Philip stroked Josh's hair, soothing the baby vampire. "You'll stay with me, right, Josh?"

He nodded, but shifted restlessly toward the nearest of Evans's men. "I'm hungry. Let me eat."

"A little more, my son. Just a little." Philip stroked Josh's back lovingly as the boy leaned over to the man's neck and broke the skin with his new fangs.

Kelsey buried her head in her hands. She'd had enough. This was her fault, but she couldn't watch anymore. "Will they die?"

Philip placed a hand on her shoulder, and she let him leave it there. One of his icy fingers stroked her cheek. "No. Not by our hands. Evans might not let them live."

"Why would he kill his own men?"

"Because they failed. He doesn't tolerate failure." He eased her hands away from her face. "I could be wrong. He might simply demote them." He shook his head. "Does it matter? They'd have killed us without thinking about it. That's what they planned to do if we didn't agree to work for them."

"I know. That doesn't justify murder."

When he glanced at Sabatino, she said, "You had no choice. It was kill or be killed." The sound of Josh's slurping intruded on her consciousness, and she cringed. "Has he had enough? Because I don't know how much more of this I can take." She met Philip's gaze with her imploring one. "Please. Make it stop."

"It'll be all right," he said, but he nudged Josh gently away from the man.

A cell phone buzzed, the sound coming from Sabatino's direction. Eyes wide, Kelsey latched onto Philip's arm. "Oh, God, it's probably Evans."

"Go get it and bring it here," Philip said. "I'll buy us some time."

She scrambled to her feet and rushed to the dead man's side. Wrinkling her face in disgust at the sight of Sabatino's mangled head, she focused her gaze on his jacket pocket from where the sound emanated. When her fingers grasped the item, she pulled it out and rushed it back to Philip. Anxious to get it out of her hands, she almost threw it at him.

Philip released Josh but ordered him to sit still. To Kelsey's horror, her boy, her baby, licked blood from his lips and swallowed, a satiated sigh escaping him as he nodded his compliance.

After a glance at the call display, Philip held up a finger, requesting their silence, and answered the call, turning it on speaker.

"Yeah." His voice sounded eerily similar to Sabatino's.

"Where are you?"

"Done."

"They all dead?"

"Yeah."

"Dwayne? He away?"

"Yeah."

"What the hell's wrong with you? Tell me what happened? Belanger's dead? The woman? The kid?"

"Yeah. I told you." Philip's voice didn't sound exactly like Sabatino's that time, but it was still close enough. She hoped Evans ended the conversation soon.

Josh stirred, restless once more. He licked his lips, wiped them with his sleeve, and mewled like a kitten. Kelsey implored him with her eyes to stay quiet, but he never even glanced in her direction. His gaze locked in on one of the two remaining men he hadn't tapped yet for blood.

Philip held a finger to his lips and shook his head. Josh settled for the moment.

"What was that noise? Where are you?"

"Café. Cleaning up. Gotta go."

"Fine." Evans sounded dubious, but he seemed to be buying the ruse. "Call me when you're done." The phone went dead.

Philip wiped the phone of prints, tossed it onto the floor next to the unconscious men, and met Kelsey's gaze. "Evans wanted us all dead. He doesn't know Sabatino tried to get us to work for him."

"I don't understand."

"He expected Sabatino to verify our deaths when he called, but Sabatino tried to force us to work for him."

Confused, Kelsey asked, "Why would he do that? Why not just do what Evans wanted?"

Philip shook his head. "I don't know. But it's possible he wanted to break away from Evans."

"With us?"

"By letting us live, we'd owe him. No doubt he was getting around to making us realize that."

"Then why shoot Josh? I'd never agree to work for him after that."

"Maybe he changed his mind. Maybe he planned to kill you and Josh but force me to work for him in exchange for my life."

"Didn't he know you'd react the way you did? My God, you're a vampire."

"It wouldn't be the first time humans underestimated my powers. He thought he had everything under control." He scanned the room. "We've got to get out of here before the cops show up. That broken door will attract attention sooner or later, and some Good Samaritan will call it in."

"My entire life was in this store. What am I supposed to do now? They'll be looking for us. Blair …" She couldn't continue. Her ex-husband would be frantic with worry if she and Josh simply disappeared.

"I'm sorry. He'll have to wonder. One day, he'll accept your deaths. Or one day, you'll be in a position to contact him and tell him what happened."

Tell Blair she'd given her permission to turn their son into a vampire? She shook her head, signaling to both herself and Philip that this would never happen. "God, he'll always wonder, and it'll torture him for the rest of his life. But it would be far worse if he knew."

Far worse for him or for her? Wouldn't she want to know the truth if the situation were reversed and he'd had Josh turned into a vampire? Truthfully, were that the case, she wouldn't understand, and she'd hate him forever. Kelsey had to admit she'd keep this from Blair to protect herself. Someday, she might have the courage to contact him and tell him, but today wasn't the day.

"It'll protect him from Evans if he doesn't know where we are," she said. That much, at least, was true.

"Yes, it would," Philip replied. "Now, where are the store cameras? We need to erase them."

She shook her head. "Sabatino made me turn them off when they brought me here."

"Okay. One less thing to worry about." He stood, and after telling Josh to stay put, he picked up the gun he'd grabbed from one of the unconscious men, the gun he'd shot Sabatino with. He wiped it clean of prints and then put it into the owner's hand. After slapping the goon's face gently to wake him, Philip mesmerized the man with a gaze and murmured soft words into his ears. The vampire left the thug sitting dazed on the floor and, one by one, woke each of the other three men. After he'd finished with the last one, he said, "Call 9-1-1 on the shop's landline, Kelsey. When they answer, set the receiver down and walk away."

She did as he requested, and when she finished, Philip pulled Josh to his feet and waved for Kelsey to follow them. Together they left the store for what Kelsey assumed was the last time.

# CHAPTER 41

Since it would be too dangerous to go to her apartment, Philip didn't let Kelsey go there. He made her leave both her cell phone and Josh's inside the store behind the counter. Philip didn't tell her, but the police would declare Josh dead based on the amount of blood the boy had spilled onto the floor and the bullet they'd find that had torn into and out of him. The mystery would be what had happened to his body and to his mother. Likely, they'd consider her missing and presumed dead after interrogating the men left behind.

One man, at least, would be charged with killing Sabatino, and Sabatino would be identified as Josh's killer. Ballistics would match the appropriate guns with the corresponding bullets, and the only prints on each would be the owner's. Philip's immediate problems were two-fold. One was the question of what he should do about Evans, who'd probably figure out what had happened. He'd know Philip, and perhaps one or both humans, had survived this encounter. Evans wouldn't go to the police about it, but he'd start a hunt for Philip, drawing the logical conclusion that if he found the vampire, he'd find the humans or at least news of them.

Two, while he'd told Kelsey she couldn't go home again, the same held true for him as well. He also couldn't return to his business—at least not right now. Since Dwayne had sold his share to Evans, it made Evans Philip's partner, something he didn't want to think about, but which he had to face sooner or later. If he disappeared for longer than seven years, Evans could declare him dead and take ownership of the entire enterprise.

*Tabarnak. That's why he wanted me dead.*

If Evans bought out Dwayne, his next move would be to buy out Philip, but when he'd continued to search for his daughter, it was simpler to just have him killed over it and inherit the rest of the business. He glanced at Kelsey, who trudged along on his right.

Her shoulders drooped. Blood from her scraped and torn wrists had smeared on her jeans. As usual, the scent drew him, but not enough to make him come close to losing control. He'd have to keep a close eye on Josh to make sure the boy didn't decide to use her as a midnight snack. On the plus side, her weariness made her more pliable than usual, and he appreciated the nice change. Her stubborn independence amused him, most of the time, but right now, he needed her to listen and accept his commands. He preferred not to force compliance, so a more quiescent Kelsey was a blessing.

Philip turned to Josh. "You up for a little speed? Test out those new vampire powers?"

The words brought Kelsey to an abrupt halt, and she clamped a hand onto Philip's shoulder. "What are you doing?"

"We need to hurry. I want him to keep up with me while I carry you vampire-style."

"Where are we going?"

Clearly, she'd gotten a second wind. Just his luck. With a deep, exasperated sigh, Philip said, "Can you trust me? This once?"

She planted her feet and put her hands on her hips in that enraged posture she often used. "I've done nothing but trust you since you walked into my store searching for Dakota." She stared in Josh's direction. "And look where it's gotten us."

The accusation behind her words stung, but he tried to push past the hurt. Of course she'd blame him. Why wouldn't she? Most of this was his fault, if you drilled down to the core of it. He never should've fallen for Annabelle, but he'd be damned if he'd take full responsibility. They'd have to argue about it another time though. Right now, he needed to get them to safety.

He stared into her eyes. "I don't want to hypnotize you, but I will if you don't listen to me."

The internal struggle to pull away from his gaze reached her face, but he held her. Her eyes kept their awareness. He refused to put her under unless she left him no choice.

"Listen to me."

She stopped struggling, but her will remained her own, and he could tell she knew it. "I'm listening."

"I have to train Josh. If we had more time, I'd do it gradually. As it is, I have to do it on the fly while keeping you both safe." He stuck out an arm, halting Josh with a hand to the boy's chest. "Keep your distance from the human, son."

Kelsey's voice broke as she said, "Why do you keep calling him your son?"

"He's my boy now. I'm his father. His vampire father. He needs to hear it. He needs to imprint on that." He sighed again. "I don't have time to explain everything to you. I'm doing the best I can."

She slowly raised her hands and placed one on each of his shoulders. "I'm sorry. This has been unbearably painful for me. I don't know what it's like for you—whether you hate that you made him one of your own or you love it." She closed her eyes. When she opened them again, he saw only compassion. "I'll trust you. You're my son's new father, and you know what's best for him—for us—right now. Do what you have to do."

He softened his expression. "Thank you." He scooped Kelsey up in his arms, and she squealed a little as he did. "You okay?"

She nodded.

"Josh." His voice was sharp, commanding, and the boy snapped to attention.

"Stay close. You ready to move? Keep your eyes on me and follow my footsteps."

"Yes, Father."

Philip sucked in a breath on the word "father." It reminded him too much of Dakota. From Josh's lips, it seemed appropriate. He wasn't Josh's dad. Josh had a dad, even if the boy never saw Blair again. Philip was his vampire father, and the word father reflected the formality and lack of emotional closeness inherent in that relationship.

After calculating the route to his destination, Philip hugged Kelsey to his chest and sped off into the night, his new son following close behind.

# CHAPTER 42

He landed them in a clearing near a cabin he owned in the middle of Algonquin Forest, an area that used to be a national park. Now it was home to the types of hypernaturals who preferred to live alone in the wilderness. Philip had purchased the cabin here at the turn of the twenty-second century, but rarely visited—only enough to keep the environment from reclaiming it. He'd bought it under another name for such a moment as this—not that he'd expected to have to disappear, but he'd learned early in his vampire career that life could change from one moment to the next. Mostly, he'd learned this from dealing with types such as Evans, who'd certainly made more than one person or creature disappear—voluntarily or not.

Philip set Kelsey on her feet and commanded her to wait outside while he and Josh verified no one was inside.

"I haven't been here in a while," he said.

"Well, you're not leaving me out here by myself."

She strode up to the front door and tested the doorknob. "It's locked." She stepped back and eyeballed the windows. "No broken windows on this side." She waved at the door. "What are you waiting for?"

He sighed, something he noticed he did frequently when she spoke. From his pocket, he pulled out a key ring loaded with at least a dozen keys. He fumbled through each one until he found the one for the cabin's front door. "At least step back while I unlock it, and let me and Josh go in first."

Kelsey glanced at her son and moved out of his way as he brushed past her. He wrinkled his nose, and saliva dripped from the corners of his mouth as he caught her scent, but he behaved himself and didn't make a move in her direction. It would be a challenge to keep the kid from attacking his mother, but Philip had no choice. Mother and son both had to stay with him or risk death at Evans's hands or arrest for accessory to murder by the cops.

Added to that, Philip had broken the law when he'd turned Josh into a vampire. New vampires could only be made after applying for a permit, getting agreement from the appropriate councils, and going through a waiting, or cooling-off, period. The red tape related to the process made it a headache, and for good reason. Once the deed was done, there was no going back.

Perhaps the vampire and human councils would accept the life or death excuse, but Philip doubted it. It was against the law to turn a human to prevent death, or most humans would use that excuse. Many tried anyway, in the years since the unmasquing. Few received the permit to do so. The penalty for a human who turned into a vampire without the requisite permits was life in prison—which meant eternity, since vampires lived forever unless they were executed. The penalty for the vampire who turned a human without the requisite permits was death. In their situation, Kelsey would end up in jail because Josh hadn't had a say in his turning and so was innocent of the crime. Philip, however, would end up dead.

He'd known this when they'd made the decision for Josh and assumed Kelsey did as well. She'd wanted to save her son. For her, the risk was understandable. Philip had no idea why he'd jeopardized his existence for a couple of mortals. Did he do it because he cared or because he believed they'd never get caught? Or because he craved a child who'd replace the one he'd lost to the fae, the one he'd neglected all her life? It was a good question, and one he had no answer to as he searched his cabin, poking into closets and shadowed alcoves.

It didn't take long to search the place, and the lack of any intruder's scent and the layers of dust on all the furniture verified it remained untouched since he'd last entered it.

"We'll have to clean it up," he commented. It wouldn't take long. The cabin had two bedrooms, a bathroom, a living and dining area, and a kitchen. Solar panels supplied electricity and water was pumped from a drilled well. They were, essentially, off the grid.

"I'll do it," Kelsey said.

Philip flashed a smile at her. "I'll let you."

He checked that he'd shut and bolted the door and that all the windows were secure. While the darkness didn't bother the vampires, who could see in the dark as well as any cat, Kelsey would have trouble, so Philip closed all the curtains and flipped on a lamp in the living room.

"I hope you're prepared to rough it. It's nothing fancy."

"We'll manage," Kelsey replied. "But what will we do for food?" Her voice quavered as she spoke, and Philip knew she pictured the two vampires feeding on her.

"Don't worry your pretty head. You won't end up our blood slave, darling."

She sucked in a horrified breath at that. "You can be so disgusting. Can't you stop and think before you speak?"

He almost chuckled at her distress—she took things so seriously—but he followed her advice and stopped to think first. "Sorry. Vamp humor. I'll take care of getting the food. Josh can help me. But we're stuck here for a while."

She frowned. "How long?"

Josh, who'd wandered restlessly around the cabin checking out his surroundings, stopped in front of Philip and poked his finger at Kelsey. "Will she be here the whole time?"

"She has to stay here. We all have to stay here together," Philip said.

"I can smell her. You told me not to feed on her, but I'm hungry again."

"Josh." It came out a gasp of anguish, and Kelsey sounded close to tears.

Philip kept his gaze on the young vampire. "I'll take you out. You'll feed."

When Kelsey cried out, Philip raised a hand to stifle her. "On animals. We're deep in the forest. We can hunt game."

"That's fine for you." She crossed her arms over her

243

chest.

"Don't worry. We'll figure it out. I can get food for you."

"At risk to yourself." She shook her head. "What have we done? Oh, God, what have we done?"

Philip put his hands on Josh's shoulders. "Go into the master bedroom and get some rest. We'll look for food after I have a word with your mother."

Josh frowned. "I'll still hear you from the other room. I can't help but hear you. And I'm not tired."

"Just leave, please. We need the privacy. Your presence is a distraction for your mother." He turned Josh and, aiming him at the bedroom, gave him a small push. "I'll come in momentarily."

With a final glance at Kelsey, Josh crossed the room. He halted in the bedroom's entry and turned to her. "I know you, who you are. I just don't care what we were to one another." He entered the room and shut the door behind him.

Looking stricken, Kelsey collapsed onto the sofa in front of the stone fireplace, buried her face in her hands, and sobbed.

\*\*\*

Complete silence made Kelsey raise her tear-stained face to meet the vampire's gaze. Compassion showed in his eyes, and she wondered why her son felt none. Did all new vampires lose the ability to empathize? Did they all lack a conscience? If so, she and Philip had made a horrible mistake unless he could somehow teach Josh to recover what he'd lost in the transition. Horrified, she realized Philip would've known this. Yet he hadn't warned her, and he'd turned Josh anyway.

She stood, throwing her shoulders back and her chest out. "You knew what would happen to him, what he'd become, but you went ahead and did it."

His expression darkened, and his fangs appeared. "You wanted me to save him, and we ran out of time. We made a split-second decision. You won't put this all on me. You knew the legal consequences to me should they arrest me for turning him, yet you were willing to risk my life to keep your son with you."

She gasped, and her eyes grew wide, terror flooding through her.

"Willful ignorance is no protection in the eyes of the law. Don't tell me you didn't know I'd get the death penalty for this."

She gulped, and her whole body went numb. "I-I forgot. I forgot. Oh, my God. They'll execute you." Why had he done this insane thing? Why even present the option to her when it cost him so much?

"They'll jail you, darling. We're both in it deep."

"Why would you risk your life for us?"

He shrugged.

She studied him. He looked so calm and unperturbed when he ought to fall apart. A weight settled onto her shoulders. She'd owe him forever for this.

When he remained silent, she spoke again, but this time, softened her voice and removed the anger and accusation from it. "But you knew he wouldn't be Josh anymore. I didn't. My son loves me. This thing you created"—she waved a hand at the bedroom—"feels nothing for me."

"I'm sorry. It'll have to be this way for a while, but it'll change. I wouldn't have done this if I thought it would destroy your life or the relationship you had with your son forever."

He sounded so certain she relaxed, letting some of the tension ease out of her shoulders and back. A lump that had formed in her throat disappeared. "Then what will we do?"

"Right now? Get food. Josh and I likely won't return until morning. I've got a gun I can leave you, as well as a talisman you need to wear at all times to shield you from magick trackers. A mage could locate us unless we protect ourselves."

"You have that here?"

"Yes. I have enough for each of us." He didn't elaborate. "Keep the doors and windows locked at all times. We're probably not the only vamps in the forest, though most of the inhabitants in these woods keep to themselves." He glanced at the bedroom. "But I don't trust any of them alone with a human."

Not knowing what else to say, she said, "I'll be fine."

She could try and get some sleep. If she managed it, they might even be home when she woke. Inside, she didn't believe it. Kelsey dropped to the couch again and braced herself for a long night ahead.

# CHAPTER 43

A sound woke Kelsey, who'd fallen asleep on the sofa. Bleary-eyed, she sat up and listened. Her heart pounded, and sweat broke out on her neck and back though the cabin was chilled. She'd built a fire after Philip and Josh had left, but it was out.

There it was again—and it sounded like a … dog's bark?

In darkness, she stood, padded to the window in her stocking feet, and peered outside. Nothing stirred that she could see, but seeing anything was difficult without even a moon for illumination.

Then she spotted it: a small animal, gray against the deeper black. It dragged one of its hind legs, and yapped and barked with fear as it inched toward the cabin. Should she bring it inside? Philip had told her to keep the door closed and locked. The poor puppy was in trouble, and it was such a little thing. It certainly couldn't harm her, but whatever had injured it might still be around.

She tiptoed to the front door and unlatched it.

Pressing her ear against the solid wood, she listened, but could hear only the pants and growls of the dog. *The hell with it. Probably a fox or coyote chased it here. I can handle that.*

Kelsey slipped on her shoes, wrenched open the door, dashed outside, and snatched the dog into her arms. A rustle in the trees behind her made her spin around and face the forest.

A naked man stepped into the clearing, his stride purposeful, his body muscled and beautiful in the faint starlight. His expression terrified her. He exuded rage, and when he spotted Kelsey with the dog in her arms, he ran at her.

She froze for a moment, and by the time she made the decision to *run, for God's sake, run*, he'd caught her by the arms.

"Give me the dog."

She couldn't speak; she could only gape at him, wide-eyed and trembling. Her legs gave out, but he held her in such a tight grip she dangled limply in his hands. Yet she kept her hold on the dog, pressing him to her chest.

Finally, she managed a faint gasp. "Let me go."

He laughed. "If I let you go, you'll fall on your face and crush my dog."

His laughter and his words had the strength returning to her knees, and she set her feet on the ground and steadied herself. "I said, 'Let me go.'"

She tried to wrench her way free, but he was too strong for her. Without looking down, because she didn't want to telegraph her moves and because he was naked, she thrust a knee up.

Not only strong, he was also agile, and he dodged the strike. With one hand, he continued to hold her arm. The other, he placed around her throat, lifting her to her toes as he cut off her air. "Try that again. Please."

She gagged and her bladder threatened to release. The dog, who growled at the man even as it trembled as much as Kelsey did, almost fell from her arms.

The man released his grip on her throat and relaxed his hold on her arm, allowing her to steady herself. She hauled in a painful breath of air and gasped until her breathing regulated.

When she had her breath back, she asked, "Who are you? What do you want?"

"I want the dog." He peered into her face as if examining her. "What are you doing here? Where's the vampire?"

What should she tell him? He knew Philip, clearly, but how? Were they friends? Enemies? It wouldn't surprise her to learn Philip was friends with a weird naked guy. She'd assumed the vampire was hetero, but perhaps …

"Are you his lover?" The words were out before she could silence them.

He spat on the ground. "Of course not."

Enemies then. Probably. Was there anyone alive the vampire hadn't pissed off?

"Why are you chasing this poor dog?" She looked down at the pup in her arms and cuddled it close to her. Dirt and blood matted his white fur, but she recognized it as a west highland terrier. Her heart melted, and she pressed her lips to its sweet head and kissed it.

The man released her so suddenly she stumbled but caught her balance and steadied herself.

"I'm trying to save it, but the damn thing took off."

"Save it from what?" She scanned the clearing and

the surrounding trees nervously. If this guy wasn't what had wounded the animal, whatever had could be nearby.

"Druids. They wanted to sacrifice it. I saved it, but it jumped from my arms. I had to chase it."

If that was true, perhaps he wasn't evil or dangerous. Before she could stop herself, she looked him up and down, scanning his nakedness from the top of his curly brown hair, down his massive chest and biceps, to his impressive male assets, then below, to his solid, muscular thighs, calves, and surprisingly well-manicured feet. When she caught herself scoping him out, the blood rushed to her face and she averted her eyes.

He laughed again, but it sounded friendly rather than mocking this time. "Give me the dog."

"What will you do with it?"

"Take him home. Clean him up. Bandage his wounds. He almost chewed his leg off trying to escape the leg trap he'd sprung."

"How did you find him?" Suspicion laced her tone. She refused to hand the dog over to the guy just because he claimed to want to help it. For all she knew, he was one of the so-called druids.

"We're of a kind," came the soft reply.

"What does that mean?"

"I'm a lycan. I could hear his suffering and followed it to the trap. The druids hunt animals in this area. They caught this terrier. It ran away when I removed the leg trap, and I shifted and chased after it." Before she could ask, he answered her question. "I have no idea what a dog who's obviously a house pet was doing in these woods."

"Would they really use it in a sacrifice? A puppy?"

He shrugged. "They need an animal. I don't think they care what kind."

She didn't want to believe that, but she had to accept what he told her. What else could she do? Accuse him of lying? He'd just deny it. "Do you live around here?"

"Yes. The vampire knows where."

"What's your name?"

"No names."

"But you have a name, don't you?"

"I'm not giving it to you."

"Where do you live?" She crushed the dog to her chest, and it whimpered and struggled. "I'm sorry, sweetie." She loosened her grip.

"You don't need to know that."

"Then I won't give you the dog."

"I can take it from you by force."

"If he's not your dog, why don't you leave him with me?" She didn't know how Philip would react to that—or Josh, for that matter. Would they want to suck its blood? Oh, this was horrible. The poor dog. She couldn't let anything happen to it.

"And let you feed it to the vampire?"

"Of course not. I wouldn't let him do that. I'll give you the dog, but you have to tell me where you live so I can check on you—him."

"You're staying here?" Now his voice sounded dubious. "A human? You a blood slave?" He peered at her throat and surprise flashed across his face. "You're not a blood slave."

"No."

"But you're staying here with the vampire?"

"Yes."

He stroked a finger down her cheek. "You'd best be

careful. Your future here is uncertain."

She smacked his hand away. "What does that mean?"

"These woods aren't fit for humans. They're filled with those that want to eat them or use them."

"I have no choice." When he didn't reply but stared at her as if waiting for her to elaborate, she said, "It's not your business why I'm here. Like you, I have my reasons."

He tilted his head. "All right. We both want to protect the dog. You don't trust me, and I refuse to leave it with a vampire."

"I can bandage him here."

"Fine. When do you expect the vampire to return?"

"Soon." She lied because she had no idea where Philip was or when he'd return, but she figured if the lycan believed the vampire could appear at any moment, he wouldn't harm her and he'd leave quickly.

"Then we'd better hurry."

## CHAPTER 44

The lycan worked quickly once Kelsey, who refused to allow him into the cabin, retrieved everything they'd need to clean and dress the wound. As they worked, she questioned him—or tried to.

"How long have you lived here?" Kelsey asked.

"Years." The lycan gave her a side-wise glance and didn't expand on that.

"How old are you?"

He grinned. "Years."

She gave an exasperated huff. "What difference does it make if you tell me how old you are?"

"I prefer to remain mysterious."

She shrugged. "Fine. Keep your meaningless secrets. It's not as if I'm pumping you for information. I'm just making conversation."

"I'm not much of a conversationalist." He deftly cleaned the dog's cuts, and the puppy patiently let him, offering puppy licks in what Kelsey assumed was gratitude for the help. He was such a cute little dog she almost wished she could keep him. But the lycan was right: the vampires would probably consider him a tasty treat.

Once the bandages were on, she plucked him from the lycan's arms. "I want to say goodbye before you take him away." A wash of grief flooded her, and she didn't understand why. She'd only just met the little dog, but she struggled to let him go.

"We should name him." She peered up at the lycan and found him smiling indulgently at her.

"Okay. Name him."

She studied the dog. With a jolt, she realized he was identical to the dog on the Fool card she'd drawn from Chase's tarot deck.

"Fool. Let's call him Fool," she said, her voice hoarse with emotion. He'd certainly behaved like a little fool. Somehow, he'd gotten lost in this dratted forest, triggered a trap, and, when the lycan released him, ran from the one person who would help him. As the card also suggested, this was a new beginning for him. *And for me.* The card had been about her future, after all.

"All right. Come on, Fool." Gently, the lycan pried the puppy from her arms. "I should go now. Before they come back."

"Yes," she whispered, still unwilling to let the puppy leave. He was hers, wasn't he? She'd drawn the Fool card. Wasn't this some kind of sign? But he couldn't stay, so she simply said, "Goodbye, Fool" and kissed the top of his furry head.

The lycan bid her goodnight. "Stay in the cabin. Never go out alone. Don't even come out into the yard if the vamps aren't home. Understood?"

She didn't understand, but agreed anyway because

if a naked man cautions you, you should probably heed the warnings. "Understood."

"Then go inside and lock the door."

She resented him ordering her around but then realized that if she stood out here and watched him go, she'd be alone outside in the dead of night. Kelsey hurried up the steps and into the house, waving a final farewell as she closed the door.

*Wonder if he'll get dressed when he gets home?* She suspected that when no one was around, he let it all hang out. She went to the window to watch him leave. By the time she peered out, he'd disappeared into the forest. She stood, staring into the darkness. *What the hell happened to my life?*

\*\*\*

Fire engulfed Blood Shots, flames licking from windows that had blown out during the explosion. Josh watched, eyes wide. Next to him, Philip stood, his heart—or what passed for one in a vampire—breaking at the sight. In the distance, sirens wailed. Someone had called it in.

"Let's go." Philip hoisted a duffel bag filled with booze and food from the bar onto his shoulder and motioned for Josh to pick up the bag he was to carry. This one, too, had food and booze. Philip also carried a satchel filled with all the cash from the bar's safe.

When arson investigators sifted through whatever remained, they'd deduce the fire had been deliberate, but Philip counted on that. He and Josh had stolen Evans's car and allowed the cameras to pick up the license plate. If nothing else, the syndicate head would have a lot of questions to answer. No doubt that, since he was part owner, they'd search for Philip as well. Dwayne, too, would be at the top of the suspect list.

Philip wondered where his partner had gone, but it was only fleeting curiosity. Dwayne was well in the wind by now. He could be anywhere. At least the traitor wasn't getting away with what he'd done. The police would hunt for him.

Next, they returned Evans's car to his house. A vampire's life had many perks. Cameras picked up the car, but if Philip moved fast enough, nothing would show up on video. Most people believed vampires had no reflections, which was false, but that rumor had grown from seeds of truth. Speed made them difficult to see with the naked eye and on video recordings. Hypnosis took care of the rest. The guards would remember Evans behind the wheel.

"Where are we going next, Father?" Josh asked.

Philip put an arm around the boy, who'd patiently followed every one of Philip's commands throughout the long night. "Home. To the cabin," Philip replied.

"That cabin's really our home?" Josh wrinkled his nose, obviously displeased with the news.

"For now. We've got to regroup, to help you adjust. We all need to disappear for a while, and we should be safe enough there." He hoped. "Your mother will need you to spend time with her."

"I feel nothing for her." Concern laced Josh's voice, which was a good sign. He held onto the memories he had of their relationship, and his lack of emotion over his lost life troubled him even if losing that life didn't.

"You will, in time." Philip patted Josh's back. "You'll have a whole new life."

Josh adjusted the strap of the bag slung over his shoulder. "I'm ready. I think I'll enjoy being a vampire."

They vanished into the night without a trace.

### 

Can't wait to dive into more tales from the unmasqued world? Chase Spenser's day—and possibly his career— is ruined when a demon appears during his potions exam. Who's behind the act, and why would they want to sabotage Chase? Read the next magickal installment, *The Magician: Infinity's End.*

If you enjoyed *The Fool: New Beginnings*, won't you please take a moment to leave me a review?

# ABOUT THE AUTHOR

Val Tobin lives in Newmarket, Ontario, with her husband, Bob, and Scully, their cat. After ten years in the computer industry programming web and software apps, she now spends her days writing, reading, editing, and searching for the perfect butter tart. Her educational background includes a diploma in Computer Information Systems from DeVry Toronto, a B.Sc. in Parapsychic Science from the American Institute of Holistic Theology, a M.Sc. in Parapsychology from AIHT, Reiki Master/Teacher certifications, and Angel Therapy Practitioner® certifications.

I really appreciate you reading my book!
Visit my website and sign up to receive my newsletter:
www.valtobin.com

# OTHER BOOKS BY VAL TOBIN

## Fiction

### Paranormal Sci-Fi Thrillers

*The Valiant Chronicles* Series

*Earthbound* (prequel): A spirit becomes earthbound after refusing to cross over in order to solve her murder and prevent more deaths, some of which might be predestined.

*The Experiencers* (book one): A black-ops assassin atones for his brutal past by helping an alien abductee escape capture.

*A Ring of Truth* (Book Two): A rogue assassin triggers an apocalypse when he attempts to rescue a group of alien abductees.

*The Valiant Chronicles* books are also available as a complete set in e-book and paperback.

### Romantic Suspense

*Injury*: A young actress at the height of her career has her personal life turned upside down when a horrifying family secret makes front-page news.

*Gillian's Island*: A socially anxious divorcée confronts her greatest fears when she's forced to sell her island home and falls for the dashing new owner.

*About Three Authors: Poison Pen*: Three wannabe authors suffering from various mental disorders find love in unexpected places when they interfere in the investigation of a colleague's murder.

*Forever Young: You Again*: Complications arise when an accounting tech is assigned her former lover as a client and his company's previous financial controller is found dead.

### Paranormal Romance

*Walk-In*: A young psychic woman fights an attraction to a handsome but sceptical novelist while she battles a power-hungry sorcerer determined to make her his next conquest.

### Horror Suspense

*The Hunted: A Storm Lake Story*: A monster hunter revisits her terrifying past while helping a reporter uncover the origins of Storm Lake's creatures. A stand-alone sequel to the short story "Storm Lake," *The Hunted* takes place twelve years later.

## Urban Fantasy

*Tales from the Unmasqued World* Series

*The Fool: New Beginnings* (book one): A newly divorced woman suffering a midlife crisis gets involved in the search for a missing half-vampire teen.

*The Magician: Infinity's End* (book two): After getting expelled for setting a demon loose on campus, a student mage searches for the real culprit and finds his troubles have only just begun.

*The High Priestess: Persephone's Return*: Stuck in the spirit world, Jaycie struggles to find a way out. But others want to keep her there forever. Will she make it out of Hades alive?

## Nonfiction

*Angel Words* by Doreen Virtue and Grant Virtue
Val contributed a story to Doreen and Grant Virtue's
*Angel Words: Visual Evidence of How Words Can Be Angels in Your Life*